FLUCTUATION IN DISORDER

Susan Maxwell

Bibliothèque des Refusés

First published in 2023
by Bibliothèque des Refusés

ISBN 978-1-7396037-2-4

'Necrologue' was first published in
Necrologue: The Diva Book of the Dead and the Undead
(ed. H. Sandler, Millivres-Prowler 2003)

OTHER BOOKS BY SUSAN MAXWELL
Hollowmen
And the Wildness
Good Red Herring
A Wild Goose Hunt

www.biblioref.com

Susan Maxwell has had short stories and poetry published in magazines and anthologies; has had one novel (*Good Red Herring*) published by Little Island Books, and a further three (*Hollowmen*, *And the Wildness*, and *A Wild Goose Hunt*) independently published; has served on fiction and non-fiction juries for the British Fantasy Awards, given a paper (vaguely PhD-related) on archives as Gothic spaces at the Past as Nightmare conference in 2022; reviews regularly for *Inis* (the magazine of Children's Books Ireland); is influenced most by speculative and modernist fiction, being particularly fond of Flann O'Brien, Calvino, Beckett, and Woolf. When not writing, or painting, or being an archivist, the author can be found in the vegetable patch, listening to music, reading books, watching old detective series, or catching up on sleep.

Praise for *And the Wildness*

"Gorgeous and hilarious and profound." *Siobhán Parkinson*

"A universal adventure story that riffs off Irish and Norse mythology…accomplished, intelligent, deeply witty and import-ant…it assumes a thoughtful and imaginative and intelligent reader." *anonymous editorial reader*

Praise for *Good Red Herring*

"Imagine a book like a Pogues concert! Chaotic, powerfully creative…littered with classic and classical Irish references all united in a glorious cacophony of intense delight and beauty." *Nigel Robert Wilson*

"I can picture a teen Neil Gaiman being engrossed by this, as it has the oddest atmosphere... The nearest comparison I can think of is *Lud-in-the-Mist* by Hope Mirrlees meets *The Dalkey Archive* by Flann O'Brien." *Karina Clifford*

"Maxwell is to be congratulated … on her inventiveness [and] her skill in keeping such a firm grip on the interweaving strands of her narrative, entertainingly employing in the process many of the tropes of the classic noir detective story." *Robert Dunbar*

Contents

Preface

This is a collection of short stories in the same way that raked leaves in a wheelbarrow are a collection: they fell off the trees, they were scattered, and now they are collected. There's no theme. The earliest story (I think) is *Necrologue*, which was published as the title story in a 1999 Millivers-Prowler anthology, and the most recent is *Each Tether Has Its End*, finished in December 2022.

The stories might be classed as fantasy, or Gothic, or irreal, or all of the above. These genres, especially the irreal, characteristically create ambiguity, or ambivalence, and where there is ambivalence, there are questions—deeply realist questions—about how reality is constituted and prioritized. The essence of the irreal is to create a reality that convinces the writer (and, with luck, the reader) of a world in which unexplained absurdities will happen, and will not be resolved. Some of these stories, especially the earlier ones, are set in or connected to preliminary incarnations of the secondary worlds that form the backdrops to the novels *Good Red Herring* and *Hollowmen*. The more recent stories try to tread a sort of hypnagogic borderline between consensus experience and speculations about the experience of disruption by the unknown.

A word (or 169) on independent publishing. Jean Rhys exhorted writers to "keep feeding the lake" of literature, which needed both the great rivers and "the mere trickles, like Jean Rhys." The literature of an age is not only what is great, or good—or at least valued, or lionized—in that age. It includes what is not very good at all, and that which, even if great, does not fit its time, and is disregarded, pushed to the margins. It is in these margins that small and independent publishers often find gems overlooked elsewhere; independent publishing presents a further, author-driven, opportunity, and both paths offer resistance to the kind of political philistinism that hollows out and devalues the arts, humanities, and anything that does not get its primary value from commercial exchange. Many authors turn to self-publishing *faute de mieux* if they cannot get a publisher to take them on. But margins—including what Philip K. Dick called 'the trash stratum'—are, ecologically and creatively, where interesting things can happen.

Someone Had Been Telling Lies

A thing a something slapping and soggy suckering swiftly repetitive some sucker some drip some single drop of noise in otherwise silence—

Such silent silence the sheets thunder cold silence too the skin shrivels. Clusters. The moment comes round again then that same sucker same drip—

A whisper blurred voices dripping smeared out of true a windy corner maybe words blown away blocked and plots conspiracies blown apart leaves and leaf litter and bones—

That beautiful, loamy past—all rooted up, van Eyck, Dürer, Self-Portrait as a Manicured Garden, all flung to the cold winds dribbling into empty sockets pockets of emptiness Fuseli's Nightmare too. Waking in fragments this unanchored this meaningless—

> #That moment when you have no idea who you
> are
> #feartheemptymirror
> #existentialistpanic
> #whatevenismyname

Each inch of skin an ear, the very pores popping to hear, eyes bulging to see what is watching—straining every synapse and the very power of will will force that which watches become visible that lurker that eye—that eye mechanical other and the terror that *I am a dimness seen in that alien eye,* a bleb or blotch or speck or other speck too immaterial to have a name needing to be flicked away—the quaking goes on, the dread that marbles the liver, spleen, bowels, fear in a slimy paternoster, bladderwrack draping, and pin-thin frissons of immobilizing fear, thin and glittering as tinsel, palm to finger-tip, knee to toe, the breath, the scandalous whisper—

the darkness tilts and there are shapes then, and thus does the first fragment return thanks be to Christ the first fragment, the names of the shapes, those words that signify the shape and all its resonances, some solid ground to seize. Table—window—inside an apartment. There. And then there's the name, of course there's a name, personal, undoubted and treasured, the arkhē of all meaning. The apartment, now, on Liberty Row, there, it has a place. That is a good part of the city, too, another handful of reality. It is painful, this punching cold clay into shape. But the room is full of the shadows of real things and that is a start, so that the pieces of the puzzle can be clawed together. The concerto of the abyss of the self gives way to the mere aleatory composition of night: snow falling against the window, the refill of a distant cistern, the coloratura humming of a machine, snow melted and slithering from a gutter.

So, there is nothing to fear. Jae, it is Jae standing barefoot and shrivelling in the freezing green-grey twilight, here is condensation from Jae's bed-warm hands on the cold gloss paint of the windowsill. The orange glow is clearly from the sulphur streetlight. This is who lives in this apartment, on this road, this is whose teeth are starting to chatter, this is who looks out over the communal garden—sallow, everything turned to gamboge and steel and ochre, retired for the Winter now, retreated into the frozen soil or under ghostly fleece—this is who can take charge and stay standing till the cold makes every muscle and nerve manifest, shaking and aching, or turn and return to bed.

Something, some dark and speckled flicker, moves in the garden. It might be a trick of the dark, a speck in the eye. Jae drops the curtain and returns to bed.

Sound again, sound insistent shrieked and brought the grey silver light of a wet morning in this city. Jae jerked awake. Elle was on the other end of the line—in this godforsaken backwater it is a line, plaited and twisted, so too were Jae's glasses twisted, crushed and mangled by a flailing elbow.

"Jae? Chief's called a meeting. Can you make it?"

That moment when you have no idea who you are.

A dozen Jaes in the dressing-room mirrors. That a decision could not wait until the next working day was not unusual, but Jae had never been summoned. From hints wafting in hallways and coffee-queues, Jae deduced the usual chronology to be that after five years in the Institute, a person could expect the tests.

On the other hand, perhaps no-one else was available, everyone else had a plausible means of excusing themselves from devoting their weekend to unpaid overtime. They printed the management contracts on thick, cream-coloured, hand-made paper with the Institute's logo embossed on the top. Everyone signed under the line that said *meet the Institute's business needs outside working hours without recompense*, the line written by those who were above consequence. The line rang out and was bizarre. Reading historical documents that bureaucratically embed outrages of former lives, there is a moment of dissonance—how could nobody have seen it?

"Jae?"

Those moments of becoming——-

"Great. The car will be with you in ten."

Always tricky to know how to dress without knowing what environment to expect but trickier again wearing contact lenses. Mornings were bad enough without being required to stick your finger in your own eye. Dozens of Jaes turned and began the search.

The car arrived promptly, ten minutes after Elle's call. Jae was ready. The Pavlovian responses had kicked in even while the accursed contact lenses slithered and sprang away, and Jae was happy with the final selection of the heather-tweed suit with the soft warm hat and scarf that suggested an intimate weekend away interrupted. Elle had, Jae noted with jealousy, made the same type of choice but had opted for hiking clothes. Thus, though she had not hiked a mile in her life, she effortlessly brought with her an air of vitality and achievement that was both bracing and sensuous. She smiled as she got into the car, and immediately sank back, solemn-faced, as she pored over papers in her hand. Jae wondered what might be the price of asking for further information, and decided it was not worth it. They did not speak.

There was nothing to think about except the gritty contact lenses, hovering on the edge between comfort and frustration, and the sublimely luxurious car-seat. The outside of the car was black, naturally, and the windows tinted, but inside was port-wine red with a lavender-grey trim. The chrome fittings were almost clinically polished, without a single smudge.

Snapshots of the city flickered by. The darkened window gave the day a sheen of unreality. Snow was still falling and the top inch or so of the canal had frozen, so the poor were skating on it, so heavily wrapped up against the Eastern winter that they looked like pompoms or knitted balloons. The streetlights were still glowing orange. They were fading in the grey of the day.

It was only in the wealthier parts of the city, such as the quarter where Jae lived, that the City Leaders had retained the lights, still lit and quenched by city employees. There were a few cars on the road, a few hardy people on bicycles, a stray dog. When the car eased to a halt at the traffic lights, Elle muttered some scathing condemnation of the petty insistence that employees of the Institute had to obey traffic laws even when they were on official business.

Across the road, a small crowd had gathered in the snow around the wreckage of a derailed tram. The people moved about like flakes of soot. Siren lights were flashing, looking festive against the snow and the window-darkened light of the day. The tram had been travelling from the south of the city where all the housing estates were, so was probably on its way to the factories. Jae sat back again, and surreptitiously tried to ease the infernal grating of the contact lens without developing red, chafed eyes.

Something hit the car with a wet smack, as it turned off the road. The left side of the car rose, crunching, and the car purred on. It eased into the narrow aperture of the security-barrier. The parking-gates opened. The barrier lifted. The car came to a velvet-quiet stop and Elle put away her papers. Safely parked, Jae sighed, opened the car door, and said impulsively,

"Another day, another downfall."

The Institute foyer was teeming. Polished granite and varnished wood mowed into fragments the sounds of all the heavy-weights speculating with the confidence of kings:

   believe there was a document came through…
  interesting developments

        waiting for reaction from the

And the high-voiced storytellers, the humble-braggers:

     meeting didn't end till after midnight

        what will happen, of

        course, is

    when I was talking to Carrington

   in confidence of course, she did just hint

while the weft and weave of the disrupted morning was expertly mended and turned by the choir of secretaries and receptionists and security guards in chorus

  …the meeting? Go right through. …for the

  meeting? Go right through. Security will

  escort… meeting? … will escort….Sixth floor.

  Sixth floor Thank you sir…sixth floor ma'am

managing the prima donnas of chancers who, undeterred by facts, insisted on their starring narratives

   had to be there—with my background,

   of course, I—

extensive previous experience of this
kind of thing   I could have told her
doesn't like to do anything in this line
without my

And all down through every cat's cradle of words, visible from every angle like tinsel on a tree *what have you heard? What have you heard? I didn't hear about —what did he say about —Why would he think that I—that's not what she told—*

the quaking hands in pockets, the frissons of cold-palmed apprehensiveness as an eye sweeps over and stops, or not, as bottle spins and points to the subject of the scandalous whisper—

Elle was in among them in an instant. Her way was the way of the sharp stick, driven into nests and stirred about among the hornets and ants, and watch the responses, massed and fluttering. They were going to the Sixth Floor, for the love of god, the place that authorized everything, you couldn't go in unarmed. *That will have to go to the Sixth Floor,* they said, the kiss of death for any good idea, *the Sixth Floor decided that…* The huge reception hall, with its windows and bright flowers, was dazzling and Jae caught only glimpses of the receptionists in their pastel kerchiefs and hard-soled shoes. Security guards were dark shadows, gliding from corner to corner, security cameras focused their eyes and whirred.

A secretary whom Jae did not know materialized suddenly beside them, and murmured something, guiding them towards the private lift. Neither Elle nor Jae dared look at each other. It seemed crass even to scratch an itching contact lens. A moment's swish brought them to their destination, and Jae had a blurred impression of the hall with its glossy doors leading into the secretaries' vast offices. The polished secretary, still murmuring, guided them into the ante-room, where chairs were set out. Some were already occupied, and a few faces turned towards the newcomers, an indistinct murmur of insincere welcome rose briefly and quickly fell. Jae uneasily took the lead towards some empty chairs, and Elle followed. That was turned to her disadvantage, as Jae was able then to stop and have a few hurried words with those already seated, thus implying that without the inhibition of courtesy, magnificently important things might have been achieved.

Between the diffused glare of the morning's spun-sugar opalescent sky through the huge window, and the tear-forming, tic-forming abrasion of contact lenses it was hard to tell what was happening. The murmurs died away like sea over shingle when the Chief Director's door snapped open, and a dust-storm of executives bustled out, trouser-legs rasping and voices grinding down to discordant rumbles. The faces were barely recognisable, lacking some ill-defined glamour. The executives' smiles scattered round the room like flung bird-seed, seeming to arrive and leave as both advance and rear guard, with the tramping and the dead-leaf rustle of the little group suspended in the middle. The pale grey figure of Dieudonné waded out, his polished secretary, balm-glistening smile fading, disappeared.

Dieudonné's shuffling hands chafed papers together meaninglessly, raking the scrawled words in search not of instruction, fact, or reminder, but of a prop, the etiolated sign of his many responsibilities lightly borne.

"The Secretary is glad to see those upon whom evidently he can rely to have answered his call." Dieudonné's words prompt a rustle of smugness, a shifting of buttocks as though their owners were inhibited by their chairs from wagging their obedient tails. Someone had not answered; Dieudonné was fingering collars.

Jae was flicking through current rumours and gossip, to find any fragment—any expressive eyeroll or deliberately neutral expression at the mention of a name—but could dredge up nothing. There were the usual sudden absences on extended sick-leave, the nervous breakdowns, attempted suicides and members of staff who finally gave in to the impulse to stay in bed sobbing. But the routine would never prompt this gathering of Olympus.

"…fully aware of the importance of your…"

Despite Dieudonné's snorting and clearing his throat of its gummy frogs, his voice was still drowned out by the common-place bustle of the office and of the city. The phones were muted but they burred incessantly, and the chiming responses of the secretaries began to meld together in a soothing lullaby. The office staff stood up, walked about, murmured to each other, turned pages, and their fingers rattled over the keys of their computers like ice-cubes tumbling into an expensive glass. Dieudonné droned on.

"…accept, even welcome feedback, but in such scenarios when issues upstream…."

The building was always hot as an hotel, so the window was slightly open. The snow had slowed down considerably but was still falling listlessly. A soft damp ridge of it formed on the bottom of the window and every now and then the ridge calved, and a sodden fistful of snow plummeted to the ground and splattered all over the pavement beneath. There was a dual carriageway in front of the building and the dull splash and tear of wheels through half-melted snow was building in frequency as the hour approached when the shops would open. Another ambulance sped by, siren blaring.

"…responsible for total quality management…"

The assembled staff convulsed as though receiving a current of electricity. The Deputy's voice behind the closed office door escalated from self-satisfied twang to spit-lubricated rage, and every head turned instantly, then just as quickly snapped back, or remained motionless in an unconvincing pose to maintain the fiction that nothing had been heard. Dieudonné shifted his heavy shoulders backwards, and continued speaking. Jae was straining to hear the words from behind the door but there was little hope of clarity. When the Deputy became angry, he had the logic and the coherence of a toddler. Dieudonné shuffled his papers together.

"I trust we have achieved clarity about our need to respond strongly to this challenge, and to take the appropriate steps to achieve our deliverables."

He nodded briefly, and loped back to the Chief's office door. The shouting continued unabated. Dieudonné straightened his shoulders and began to reach out for the door-handle. The Deputy's voice went up by a major fifth, and Dieudonné hesitated. He turned around sharply, and with his head thrust forth and his nose tilted up he strode from the room.

Rousing as the words had been, no-one wanted to be the first to stand. Jae and Elle turned at the breath of a hand's touch, and M. Enopy whispered a vague invitation to coffee.

They sat beside the windows. All of the wood in the canteen was bright and varnished. The day outside was hazy and blue and in the grape-dark corners where the sun had not reached there was a remaining bristle of frost. Jae, Elle, and M. Enopy had all chosen espressos. The cups were antiques, Alexandra shaped and burgundy ivy-leaves dangling from the gold rim onto the pure bone-white porcelain. M. Enopy took a mouthful of coffee. He rattled the cup carelessly into the saucer and took out a cigarette.

"These people," he said, "Espresso in a teacup."

Jae combined a nod with a headshake and an eyeroll. Here and there, heads were turning at the crack of the sulphur match, the hiss of the flame and the smell of forbidden smoke. M. Enopy blew out a brisk mouthful of smoke and dabbed a few imaginary crumbs.

"Of course, it is left to us to make sure these things happen." He flicked his eyes upwards, to indicate the meeting they had just left, and smiled conspiratorially, affectionately, at Jae.

"Yes, indeed, sir."

"In fact, the truth is," he flicked ash without aim, "The

solution is simple. If the authorization form was simply—corrected, at an appropriate level, and re-issued with another signature, then—well."

"Can this be achieved?" Jae asked, attempting to match but not outreach M. Enopy's clipped, elliptical mode of speech. They made eye contact infrequently.

"Of course," the reply was immediate, "It could be. Could be. If the Head of Registry…"

Jae nodded, looking across the heads of diners towards the French doors that lead to the Directors' Gardens. M. Enopy was looking the other way, out across the spotless gravel towards the exit from the Formal Gardens.

"Can she be persuaded to sign it?"

"It would certainly simplify things," Enopy said, stubbing out his cigarette vigorously. He took another sloppy mouthful of coffee and smacked the cup into the saucer.

"The key thing here is that we don't back down. She signs, or she sees her position is untenable. The idea of—well, argument, leverage, appeals. No."

"Just hold the line."

"Good. We'll wait to hear from you, then."

Jae left first.

Each floor of the building had a kitchen area at each end, to add to the pretence that the staff were to socialize and build meaningful relationships with each other. As the delegation from the sixth floor approached the door of the Registry, Kaye Kaminsky emerged from the kitchen on the north side of the building, carrying a mug. She was an almost aggressively unglamorous—ungroomed, nearly—person approaching middle age at a steady canter. Elle looked her up and down and from the side of her mouth said to Jae,

"Like Noel Coward said, *darling, I told you to behave yourself, not dress like a fucking geography teacher.*"

Uncomprehendingly, Jae snorted with laughter, quickly

smothered.

A black jacket with a faux tapestry-pattern skirt in a faintly pre-Raphaelite green. The jacket even had shiny elbows. Kaye smiled, and Jae recognized her there and then: not who, but what. That smile. What she was, was alone on a high sea with no flags of alliance.

Her immediate willingness brought a familiarly conjoined feeling: sadness that such dark-dwelling people existed, and Schadenfreude. Scheherazade. Schadenfreude. Elle smiled delightedly and waved, beckoning; Jae heard the murmured steer, *mark me down your wingman*. Kaye approached briskly. Elle suggested that they go to the kitchen so they could be a bit more comfortable, and she scrunched her face up like a confiding hamster.

They were only on the first floor, after all. The kitchen was small, bright and cold. The table they sat at was made of reconstituted wood, moulded to mimic the Gothic carved oak and elm that had furnished the entire building at the Institute's inception but that was now on display only in reception rooms overhead. Jae sat down, opposite Kaye. Elle sat a few millimetres further back.

Jae talked, Kaye nodded and frowned, and puzzled.

"But no," she said, when her moment came to pin her colours to the mast, "No. You must know that's impossible."

She talked on. Jae nodded, fumbling a pack of index cards from an inside pocket. Inside pockets were the best. It gave everything you took from them a patina of meaning. Kaye talked on. Jae nodded and shuffled. Every now and then, Jae flicked a card over and spoke the words written on it. Teamwork makes the dream work, remember. It's a realisable abstraction. Let me give you some space for a mind-tumble. Let's look at the magnets on your thought-fridge. Sometimes Jae had the faintest flicker of worry about these cards.

The sky was clearing. The clouds that had glittered and obscured had withdrawn and were in a pleated pile on the horizon. The building faced out onto a road rebuilt after a war, and the trees were starting to shed orange and red leaves. Jae did not know what kind of trees they were. They looked exotic, a thick trunk suddenly bulging into great cushions leaking amber and sprouting a forest of thin whips. Slim-shouldered birds studded the ridges on the rooves across the road. Every now and then the silhouettes shifted, and some loose choreography was enacted, before the black shapes hunched down into waiting.

Kaye was saying something, some meandering idea, this was legal, that was illegal. She spoke in numbers, Jae noticed, arguments presented in threes, answering even the simplest assertion with "but there are two factors affecting that", limitlessly complicating, infinitely twisting, relentlessly unpacking in Mary Poppins fashion absurd objections and alternatives, obsessively disrupting what ought to be the simplest of binaries: this is wanted, will you provide it?

The birds in the middle shifted up, one flew off a chimney and butted into the line, the line disrupted and settled. The infinitesimal movements of the sun washed violet into irregularities in the snow on the rooves opposite. The snow had a crust of sparkling frost, and Jae smiled. The little darknesses looked like commas, they had a regularity that signalled but withheld meaning. They resonated and sensation responded, the sensation, a horripilation, of memory creeping on little fog-feet, itching spiky caterpillar feet, towards coherence. The regularity of the shapes in the shadowy snow would shatter into dissonance or would sound the keynote and, in the reassuring percussion of things falling into place, be resolved. In its way, it did both: recognition came but fell away into irrelevance. It had not been recognition of a thing but of an association. The violet shapes in the snow had reminded Jae of sucker marks, of a squid or other tentacled creature not usually found climbing rooves.

Finally, Kaye dropped her hands palm down on the table and looked out of the window. Her jawline was soft and slumping. She took a deep breath, in stages, as though she had been holding her breath for a long time without replenishment.

"That's that," she said.

Jae had never been into the Registry back-office before, knowing of it mainly as a name on documents and by its status of the location of a labyrinth of arcane rules and convoluted processes to answer even the simplest question. Jae had been to the Registry's service area only once, because several secretaries were inexplicably unavailable at the same time that a Divisional Chief had required a Most-Official document. The result was that Jae, bemused beyond measure, had been sent to acquire it from the Registry. A polished woman had explained patiently about the forms and the carbon-copies and the signatures; Jae instantly forgot these and was left only with the impression of a merry Clytemnestra in a glamourous blouse flinging her woven net over a doomed Agamemnon.

There seemed, Jae thought now, to be an extraordinary number of people working in the Registry. A menagerie of machines whirred and burbled in the background and Jae had the impression of a tide of people emerging from behind desks, hurrying about, lunging for phones, pushing gurneys piled high with papers and wielding unlikely and dangerous-looking implements, the nature of which was impossible to deduce. Kaye was the only person standing still amid this hustle. A pause occurred when a platinum blonde, who looked like Jean Harlow and seemed to be doing seven things simultaneously, read something from the computer screen. She said, addressing the entire office,

"DOI's looking for the latest on *Mergus octosetaceus*, apparently there may have been a sighting on the Rocas Atoll."

Everyone apart from one of the men and a bronze-haired woman looked up and looked at Kaye. Kaye nodded slowly and said,

"Send along the ACTI file—it needs to be signed for but doesn't need clearance—and add a note to say we have an F53 file. Check if we have a C-level file but don't mention it to DOI unless there's a direct question."

The movement started again, the river of people in spate once more, needing only the formal, oral stamp of permission before those who had known already exactly what they were going to have to do got on with doing it. Kaye, no longer required, looked around her desk. There was nothing to pack.

'Whose idea was this?" she asked suddenly. Jae had no idea, and so looked wise and secretive.

"Pahlavi, probably,' Kaye mused without interest, "Two-faced, back-stabbing little drama queen. Or Corfrezi, either. Reynolds, maybe. So lovely to have a choice."

She sighed again, breathing in slowly, in stages, testing an unfamiliar foodstuff.

"Can someone please run a 17DF report please?" she said to the office in general.

"A—17DF report?" Jean Harlow repeated, unsmiling, "a 17DF? Who do I run that for? Who are we taking out of the system?"

"It's for me," Kaye repeated curtly, and the blonde looked stunned. Everyone became quiet abruptly. Jean Harlow looked at Clytemnestra, no longer merry. A hirsute chap in designer casuals approached slowly, looking at each of his colleagues so as to include them in his bewilderment, his shaven headed colleague in a suit stopped in the middle of the floor, round-eyed, rolling a laden trolley to and fro as though rocking it to sleep.

"Ironically, I can still sign it," Kaye added, "M. Enopy will,

I am sure, tell you who will be in charge until I'm replaced."

She looked back at her desk. The office was a long one and silence was filling it up like air hissing into a balloon. Kaye lifted her head a little and jerked her chin aimlessly, smiling at no-one. The other staff were looking from Jae to Kaye to Elle and back again. Their expressions were mixed—Jae saw relief, anxiety and hope in probably equal parts. Kaye drew a deep breath and sighed, without regret but as though wishing her last breath to be a deliberate act.

"You can keep my things," she said to them, "It seems I'm going home."

Kaye tapped the surface of the desk, as though she thought some final gesture was needed but found that her years there could be summed up in a meaningless and forgettable rap of her fingers on what passed for furniture. She unbuttoned her jacket and walked out of the office. One or two of the staff watched her progress towards the door but heads were already turning back to their screens and trolleys and impossibly complicated machinery.

Once out in the corridor, Kaye walked briskly towards the exit to the emergency stairs. Jae's lenses were beginning to grate and scrape again, so that the passageway that was narrow and somewhat gloomy had a fractured, blurred quality that bred a kind of uneasiness, almost approaching dread. Kaye set a fast pace. The passageway was long. Most of the doors were closed but had a small aperture that, though sealed with a pane of leaded glass, allowed Jae opaque snapshots of life on the second floor: someone holding three slim volumes turning to look behind, someone carrying a tray of confections stopping to laugh vigorously, someone placing their hand over someone else's eyes.

A few doors were open, allowing out the soundtrack too. A bearded man in twin-set and pearls was dictating a letter about calculating levels of insecticides. Another man, broad-shouldered and bow-legged in a grey wool suit, was smilingly lambasting for some perceived misdemeanour a gathered group whose expressions were shifting from bland helpfulness to surprised dislike. Someone behind a screen was complaining about the air-conditioning and through the next door on the opposite side someone was cautiously, ponderously, heaving themselves up onto the radiator behind their desk.

"What are you doing?" Kaye said, stopping so abruptly that Jae and then Elle almost crashed into her, "What do you think you are doing? Do you know nothing, you great shitehawk? You can't come this way, you go back to the foyer, one of the security guards will be waiting for you."

"Both of us?" snapped Elle and Jae wondered what she had expected.

"Well, of course both," Kaye said with exasperation, "Every impediment has its shadows and every hand its puppets. How could they manage their smoke and mirrors if enantiomorphs are going to part company with themselves?"

"Where are you going, then?" Jae asked.

"Oh, for pity's sake," Kaye sighed, "Really? Look it, you had better be on your way. All the best, now. Off you pop. Mind out for the sudden monstrous crow, as black as a tar-barrel."

"All the best of what?" Elle said mockingly and Kaye laughed.

"All the best," she repeated, "All the best to all of them, and all the best from me, and all the best of fucking luck to you and Tweedledee."

She tapped her badge against the electronic lock, slipped through the waxing gap between the door and the frame, and disappeared into the dark. The hard soles of her shoes hammered the concrete steps like mouse-nails. Elle and Jae listened as to a stone thrown down a well to measure its depth. The concussion of sole to steps grew louder, fuller, more thunderous, and though at one point she clearly stopped to take off her shoes, after half a minute the striking of her steps rang out again, different now, hollow and booming.

Elle and Jae were escorted downstairs by one of the Registry staff, a tiny woman with dimples deep as wishing-wells, and seed-sized red beads sewn around the edge of her headscarf. Jae had by this time lost the ill-fitting contact lens and found that the relief from irritation outweighed the difficulty of trying to hide the need to squint. The Reception was calm again. A receptionist had taken delivery of exotic flowers, flown in that morning from the Institute's field-offices on the other side of the world, and was inhaling their perfume in a state of shut-eyed, beatific pleasure. His supervisor said something curt and he hastily looked stern and walked away to fetch a vase. There was pollen on his chin. Elle saw someone whom she recognized and gave a full-body mime of hello: bending her knees as though trying to peer through a window, waving her hand, big smile, tilting herself slightly sideways to suggest, Jae thought sourly, an unpredictable personality. Elle touched Jae's arm and said,

"Must dash. I have to say this, though, Jae. Thank you so much for all you did this morning, it means a lot to me."

"No, really, not at all, no trouble," Jae said sincerely, "Any time. You know that, I hope, Elle."

She put her head one side, to say she was touched. Just as she left, she said,

"I did wonder why everyone on the Second Floor was working."

"Ah, well, there, now," Jae said, "The heart does not stop beating even as the body sleeps. Goodbye, Elle."

Jae walked away, thrilled with the disconcerted expression on Elle's face. That inspired nullity was the perfect ending to a fruitful and meaningless morning, being resonant and sterile simultaneously. The security gates were open, Jae walked out of the HQ building and straight into the car that was already waiting. The sun was bright on the snow and the weekend city had begun to awaken.

The quickening flow of traffic obliged the car to wait at the junction. Panting on the side of the road, still there, was the stray dog they had hit as they arrived at the Institute. Its lolling tongue was crimson and silver, and its eyes were swimming with black-flecked gold. Its sides heaved shallowly, quaking in the freezing slush as it died. Through the intercom, Jae told the driver to go to Paddington's, a brunch destination that the Institute staff so favoured that no directions were necessary. On arrival, the car mounted the footpath expertly, bringing Jae right to the edge of the garden seating, so that there were only a few metres of concrete to be negotiated, and in any case they were being heated and dried so there was no threat of a tumble. There was a small commotion as the car, skidding a little as it took off, bumped one of the waiting wheelchairs, but the door of Paddington's was sound-proofed.

Jae caught the eye of the waiter and ignored the sign telling customers, in six languages, to wait to be seated. The best seat in the place, a warm corner with windows on either side, was free. Jae settled in, phone already open, to check each social media platform. Without anything to say, but wanting to be the first to comment, Jae took a quick photograph of the scene outside the window.

It was a lucky shot. The clear light spangling the snow like tinsel was so clear as to look enhanced. A perfectly timed girl in a red wool coat with a black velvet collar stopped at the traffic-lights, a perfectly painterly counterpoint to the sallow sky and the sepia of the snow, churned under wheels and marbled with charcoal grit. The whip-line of smudged circles like pock-marks on the window did not show up, and Jae sent the picture into the ether with the comment 'Happy to help', and a prompted reaction of 'feeling blessed'. Across the road were telegraph poles, draped with wires crowded with, thick with, slim-shouldered birds arranged like sheet-music for some dramatic passage, the opening to Beethoven's Fifth, Jae thought and noted down the thought, adding, *or something aggressive and*

Rachmaninov. This comparison was saved for later use, for some occasion when it would both make and give an impression.

Some melted snow slithered from a broken gutter, slapping sloppily on the window, and a small avalanche followed as something slipped on the roof and tumbled down, a grey and brown flash, a dark and speckled flicker, past the window and under the sill. The birds on the wires shifted. A familiar seagull approached on an updraft and came to earth. It paced ponderously by the wall, its head briefly visible above the windowsill. Snow spattered, and a little blood with it.

The coffee arrived, and with it the speciality of the house, a large roll with a cargo of salted bear-meat layered with cheese. The distinctive, rich stink of the meat and the spiky tang of the cheese caused its inevitable frisson of pure, or at least unadulterated, sensual pleasure, almost as great as the full-body relief when Jae took out the remaining, disorienting, contact lens. The bread was still warm. Eating the roll without smearing the sauce and the juices everywhere like a drunk eating a kebab required concentration. With no lenses, the view out of the window was blurred, and the whip-line of sucker-shaped smudges was doubled now, a spun-sugar opalescent world with its distant figures moving, featureless and ragged. It was going to be a fine day

Battle Book

COMMANDS CAME to them like waves along a curved sea-shore: a smothered rustle of cries becoming louder and clearer as they passed through the ranks. After so long—months? a year?—of battle, the images of sea that would have been on the tip of Bosco's tongue were blurred with distance. Now he thought the Commander's words more like the sparks of fire detonating along a line of gunpowder while the warriors scrambled back to safety. Beside him, Clement rose up onto her toes the better to see down the line, using Bosco's shoulder as an anchor. But she was still too short, at the same height as Bosco, to see past the high padded shoulders of the soldiers.

Finally the spark came to them, through Mill Thomas. Thomas did not speak to them, he disapproved of children at the war, but Bosco saw the way the man's body moved when the exhausted messenger, his face as pale as a seashell in the twilight, finished speaking and turned away. Thomas' shoulders sank, and his duty-stiffened spine curved into a slouch. His head bowed over his fingers fumbling with his belt, and when he had unloosed his sword and knives he sat straight down on the ground, without moving his feet, and rested his head on his knees. The army of the Earl would travel no further today but camp where it lay.

They had marched through mild summer, and that had taken them from the west coast of Hibernia, where Clement and Bosco were scions of neighbouring families obligated, through the bonds of family ties and the harsh friendliness of politics, to support the Earl. All through that march and through those early days, everyone had the energy to pick apart and judge the reasons for the war even though the assurance with which they spoke was a lie; they knew nothing. News travelled slowly.

Gossip and speculation spread like fire in dry furze, surging in sudden clouds that billowed like a murmuration of starlings, blocking out the sun. News, with some germ of fact or truth in it, was much harder come by. In the first instances it was brought by mouth from the very place where skirmishes and battles had taken place, the proof being in the memories and scars of the people who stood in halls and in public squares to tell the story of what happened. Then they fell victim to waylayers and road-side murderers, or to the forgers of maps, and instead animals —carrier pigeons, half-tamed foxes—brought scraps of cloth or vellum or paper on which the latest news was hastily scribbled.

By the time that the last cynic had been persuaded that the Aegyptians had not been lying about an invasion, not even animals were safe, and every tramp and travelling show-man was suspected of carrying news hidden among their patches and glitter. By the time that the alien army launched a first attack on Hibernian soil, it was three years after they had app-eared out of The Black and into the Aegyptian skies; messages and orders were being passed by hot-air balloons and by the ringing of bells.

Evenings descended without warning at this time of the year. Bosco and Clement huddled together beside a spreading hazel-nut bush, and the mere fact that they were now sheltered from the insistent wind let them believe that they were warm. Bosco wore a cloak given to him by his older brother, and the black wool was as heavy as if it was still attached to the sheep: once it did not get wet, his father had said as Bosco was leaving, he could survive anything wrapped in that cloak. Clement's cloak in its young day had been a warm red and was made so that it wrapped not only around her shoulders but was belted at the waist and fell in pleats over her legs. Under this she wore the same kind of brown tweed trousers, travel-stained and battered, worn by Bosco and almost everyone else in the Earl's army.

But no amount of even the best weaving could keep off a December wind in an open field. All around them, men and women hunched over the small bowls of food that were handed out to them. Lann Mac Cormac, the Commander on the Earl's behalf, always had food ready, however paltry the kitchen might be, before anything else: a full belly was better than a dry backside, she said. The field in which they had halted was small enough, fewer than ten acres, and bounded all around by a thick hedgerow, black and stark against the pearl-grey sky. Here and there were remnants of fences, woven from willow-wands and now springing loose again, and a small shelter, probably for penning sheep, had collapsed on itself.

The eastern side of the field was the most sheltered, and clustered in the lee of the snow-laden rowans and the beech trees were several sheds, a sty and a large barn. Much of the snow on the field was undisturbed, but Clement could make out the edges of vegetable plots, remnants of low brick walls and even the ruin of what looked like a small still. It had been a small farm, but someone had made the most of it, though by the looks of it, not for a few years. Bosco straightened up, and she could see him peer about into the gloom.

"No sign of a house,' he said, 'But where there's a farm there must surely be shelter for the farmer. Even a cabin."

"A cabin will fall down if it has no fire in the hearth for a year," Clement said, repeating what she had heard, and Bosco, who had seen more abandoned cabins than she, only snorted gently. He reminded her of her dog sneezing. He squinted round again.

"Maybe it is in the next field," he said, "See—the hedge is broken here and there, and this field leads straight into the next. There's a bit of a dip, maybe the cabin's there."

Clement nodded, distracted by the muffled stamp in the path behind her where the last of the soldiers were arriving. All of the snow had been trampled over and the mud and clay churned up, so the horses struggled to pull the catapult on its cart, though the catapult was one of the smallest of its type. The horses snorted and wrenched their heads about, and the men behind them shouted encouragement. The air rattled in the horses' exhausted lungs, and then clouded out as they snorted with the effort of movement; they lurched forward into the vapour of pearl.

The army had requisitioned not only horses, and the oxen that lumbered up dragging the cannon, but pigs and goats too. Bosco recognized the big boar as the terrifying beast that had belonged to his neighbours. Now the pigs were armoured like the horses, trained to be on guard at night, or to help forage during the days. The goats were guard-animals; ever since the alien army crossed the narrow sea from Aegypt it had seemed that the goats were always the first to raise the alarm. They were able to sense aliens at a great distance and tales passed from town to town about how goats, with horn, hoof and tooth, had protected their humans.

Bosco sat on the ground and peered through the brambles and grass to watch lines of legs shuffle and stamp past, made stout by many layers of wool, some with boots broken and held together with straps of leather or cloth, some without any footwear at all, but with their feet bundled up in enough cloth to make another cloak for Clement.

Two men strode the field, shoving wooden bowls of food into the hands of the waiting foot-soldiers, and Clement and Bosco scrambled further back into the hedge to eat. The sky had darkened from dove to amethyst, but it was light enough to see by, if the meat had been identifiable; they chewed thoughtfully, and agreed it must be mutton. Both avoided admitted that during war-time, it could have been dog, or donkey, or cat; Bosco's mother, a veteran of a different war, said the only thing you could be sure was that it would not be a man, a hare or a pig. But neither Clement nor Bosco would admit this possibility, feeling the other too tender-hearted to bear the thought of eating a companion animal. Thrust into the earth-coloured stew was a slice of old brown bread. Clement took a bite, then fished out the bread and held it aloft.

"I feel I have learned a harsh lesson," she said, "Even knowing that bread this foul exists."

Bosco sniffed at his, and laughed. He ate the end that had been in the stew, at least that tasted mostly of meat and onions, and he and Clement crumbled up the remainder, and scattered it out, handful by handful. The bread had been to allow them to eat the food without using only their fingers, but Bosco had a tool made for him out of horn by his father. It had a smooth spoon at one end, and a pike at the other, and he and Clement shared this, he using the two tines and she using the spoon. As they ate, a fieldfare and two blackbirds inched closer, hunger winning out over timidity. They began to peck at the crumbs. The fieldfare hopped closer to Bosco's foot, and flicked its head onto one side. The dark chevrons on its breast were swallowed up by the shadows. The marks should have served to distinguish one thrush from another but they could barely distinguish the living from the dead, so imposs-ibly thin did the bird appear.

The grass was flattened all around the edge of the field, and the birds hopped hither and thither without making any im-pression whatever on the frozen blades. The sun had not melt-ed even the snow and frost on the grass, and the earth was frozen hard beneath, hard as iron and cold as a corpse. There had been precious little daylight at all. Bosco had lost track of the days but he knew it was close to mid-winter. He looked up at the sky, trying to picture the height of the sun at midday.

"It might be today," Clement said without warning, seeing him look up.

He looked at her. She ate her last spoonful of meat and examined the spoon all over, as though in hope that another morsel might be hiding somewhere in its smooth curves.

"If you were thinking about the solstice," she said, by way

of explaining, "Today might have been the shortest day of the year."

Bosco said nothing, but, looking past Clement, put down his bowl and hurriedly stood up. Mill Thomas was striding towards him, purple cloak billowing behind him. Behind him was the Commander. Without taking his eyes off her, Bosco pulled his cap back on and straightened it, and then reached down to yank Clement's shoulder so that she would stand too. As the Commander strode past, the foot-soldiers scrambled to their feet, and then sat down again. Clement couldn't find her hat so hurriedly draped her cloak over her hair, and tried to look as though that was proper order. To his horror, Bosco saw Mill Thomas look directly at him and, so that there was no mistake, pointed and gestured for Bosco to step forward. The Commander stopped.

The Commander was middling in height and girth, and looked very like her cousin, the Earl, with high, sharp cheek-bones and deep dimples. Mill Thomas told her the names of the two children, and she nodded at them without speaking, but raising one eyebrow at Clement's unorthodox head-covering. Clement dropped a clumsy curtsey and Bosco, confused, did the same. He and Clement looked at each other, each wide-eyed with fear as to what they might have done to draw the attention of the Commander upon them.

"I am sorry to tell you," the Commander said, "Harper Gullion was killed. I think he may have been a relative of yours."

"A very distant one indeed, ma'am," Clement said, pulling herself together, "But we are sorry to hear he is gone."

There was a slight pause. The Commander frowned deeply and looked at Mill. Clement was puzzled. Even if Harper Gullion had been as close a relative to them as he was to the Earl, there was no reason for the Commander to break the news herself. Clement looked at Bosco. He was frowning too, still standing to attention, looking at Mill Thomas, hoping for guidance. Evidently Clement's answer was not the one expected or wanted. Mill said,

"I think you will find that Harper was a close relation of yours," and as Bosco shook his head, Mill raised his voice a little.

"Gullion carried the Earl's cumdach. And the book cannot walk by itself, now that he is dead."

There was further silence. The sky had darkened from amethyst to heliotrope, and snow and distance smothered the sound of the foot-soldiers walking towards the sleeping-quarters, such as they were. High above the Commander's head, Bosco could see four bright stars. He was not thinking about the Commander or Harper Gullion. He was thinking about the contents of the cumdach: about the battle-book.

Three summers ago, Bosco had travelled with his mother and his little sister to their cousins in Durrow. It had been a pleasant if tedious journey, crossing the Sionnan had been fun, and his little sister had been enthralled by the fish in the clear waters. His mother's cousin had married a cousin of the bishop's and although the reason for the visit was to see a new baby—Bosco was resigned to such trips, but he did not understand them, since all the new babies looked exactly alike—the familial connection meant a trip to the Abbey.

While Bosco stood politely by during the conversations between the adults, a monk took pity on him, and spoke to him in a low voice about the Abbey, about some of the relics, and some of the learned brothers who had lived there. Bosco responded in kind, with tales of similar abbeys and churches he had seen in his own place, though the little church in his town was not remarkable. The monk commented politely enough on what he had heard of it and asked Bosco if he would like to see the abbot's manuscript. The monk sidled up to the Abbot who was in mid-sentence, and from a hidden pocket in his robe, removed something. The Abbot, evidently accustomed to such familiarity, merely raised his arm out of the way and continued talking. The manuscript was a psalter, hardly bigger than the palm of the monk's hand, bound between wooden boards. The pages were thick, and the writing was squat.

"He carries it with him," the monk said, "so that during the day if he has a quiet moment, he can open the psalter and pray."

"I expect that the Abbot does not have many quiet moments," Bosco said, for the sake of saying something, turning over each leaf. He could not read it. He had been taught to read, and taught a little Latin, but had so little use for either in the course of his days once out of school that he was rusty. But he was enthralled by the little book. The letters were black, crisp against the buttery-white of the skin on which they were written. Gold and red and green flared out in knotted borders, around the big letters, and from the depths of pages fully covered with discs and limbs and endlessly entwined tendrils. Bosco touched his finger to the page, wondering if it was even possible to see where the pattern started and finished. It might have been the inside of some bizarre machine that the artist had created, with wheels and cogs and shafts, with arms and pistons poised waiting for a surge of steam to set them working. At the same time, though, they might have been animals, or plants; holding the book a little bit away from him, Bosco could see the shapes as birds, as the hind leg of a greyhound, the jaws of a snake.

He turned the pages carefully, only half listening to the monk's light, hoarse voice chattering amiably, until he reached the last page. He felt bereaved as he closed it.

"…plain for all to see that he had no idea how to do it, so the unfortunate saint looks exactly like a bell with little feet at the corners."

"You would have to read and write very well to create such a book," he said to the monk.

"To read and to write are different gifts," said the monk,

taking back the book, "Though if you cannot read, you must write very carefully—I have heard that carelessness has had Our Lord using scandals as footwear."

"With many worlds for the Saviour to mind, a slip of the pen will surely be forgiven."

The monk gave Bosco an astute look.

"A skill in writing can always be put to good use in a monastery. How old are you now? You left the school early, your mother said, to help you father."

Bosco nodded absently, not thinking about the monk or the divinity or even the Abbot now approaching. He was thinking of silence, and of pale skin adorned with glittering black ink, with gold and ruby and emerald colours all perfect within endless scrolls and knots.

Bosco shook his head, less to contradict what Mill Thomas was saying and more to bring himself back to the present.

"What is, or what is not, is of no concern to me," Mill was saying, through his teeth, "What matters is what is believed. People believe that the book will give them a blessing, give them the power to win against these aliens, whatever they are. It must be someone from the Earl's own family. The Commander's power has to come from the Commander herself, being in place of the Earl—the book's power has to come from elsewhere. You have a distant connection, you have a family resemblance. That will do us—you can carry the book."

The Commander held the cumdach to Bosco. It was a rectangle of silver, studded with small gems. An artist of great skill had covered every inch of the silver with engravings of knotted threads and unreal animals. In the centre there was an empty socket that had once contained a big egg of a moonstone, long lost. Bosco hesitated a second too long before reaching to take the cumdach and Mill hit him a thump on the shoulder. Bosco slipped, landed on one knee, and grabbed the little studded container out of the Commander's hand as he fell.

"The Commander has blessed her little cousin," Mill shouted; the most effective of soldiers, he could turn in an instant any chance happening into a tool to achieve the result he wanted. The Commander hastily put her hand on Bosco's head, as soldiers turned back on their walk to their beds or came back outside from the makeshift tents and shelters. Seeing what looked like a blessing or a swearing of a promise, many of them cheered and there was some scattered applause.

"Mill Thomas, you are shameless as a monkey," the Commander grumbled, as Bosco staggered to his feet. Mill shrugged.

"It has to be done. There is a strong belief—a faith, that someone must walk—"

"I know, I know," the Commander said impatiently, "Three times around the army carrying the battle-book. These are people who claim to believe in the new religion and here they are, believing exactly like the old pagans believed, in the power of objects."

"Go and tell them that, then," Mill Thomas snapped, "And then tell them to get up tomorrow morning before dawn and fight the alien army without the blessing they want."

There was a pause of indeterminate nature. Bosco could hear Clement swallowing nervously. Mill Thomas added, as an afterthought,

'Ma'am.'

The Commander shrugged.

"I'm just saying," she said, tersely, "It's illogical."

"No one on this island has seen any of the alien race that are said to have come to Earth," Mill said, "No-one knows why they are supposed to have come, what they are supposed to want, what they are going to look like, whether they have come in peace or to take what we have. But everyone lying in those tents tonight will kill and be killed, without the slightest idea why, and without any freedom to say yes or no. *That's* illogical."

"This is the book of the Red Earl?" Bosco said, before the adults came to blows, "The first Earl of—"

"Yes, and he probably would have been a lot less Red if he hadn't spent half his life sucking drink into him," the Commander said forcefully, "So don't be getting carried away by the magic of the whole thing. As soon as everyone is in their tent, hang that yoke around your neck and get you gone."

She walked away and Mill followed her. Bosco put his hands over his face.

By the time everyone was in their tent and quiet, the sky was black as the abyss. There were bright, high silver stars but it was the night of a new moon, so even with the snow, Bosco and Clement could hardly see their feet below them. Here and there were pools of amber light from candles and lanterns from the tents and the half-open doors of the derelict buildings that the quartermaster had managed to patch together, but the light clung close to its source and was of little help. The struggle against sleep had been a hard one and eventually Clement, who was a night owl and of no use in the morning hours, had sneaked away and returned with a harp slung across her back.

"I had a little chat with the drummer-boy," she said, whispering because in the frozen night-time every sound seemed to resonate, "and Harper Gullion was also—well, the harper. So I borrowed the loan of his *clairseach* to help to keep you awake."

When the tunes Clement knew best on the harp had a lulling rather than rousing effect on him, she changed to more military airs, and she played with more enthusiasm than skill. But Bosco remained awake and that, as Clement remarked through their giggles, was after all the main thing. When most of the sleeping-quarters were in blackness and the field was mostly quiet, Bosco and Clement stood up; he, as instructed, hung the leather strap of the cumdach around his neck and she, on an impulse, crossed the strap of the harp from shoulder to hip, left to right, and pushed the harp behind her.

"Let us get us gone," she said, mocking now that the Commander was safely out of earshot. They crunched off into the snow and the dark.

* * * *

Even at the time, they knew that there was no point in bickering over who had first veered away from the path, and they endured the reproachful silence that was finally broken by Bosco saying,

"As my mother would say, it could have happened to a bishop."

"That's a cumdach you have around your neck," Clement said, "A saint had the handling of that wee book. So even better than a bishop."

"True enough," Bosco said, relieved though unsurprised that they had silently forgiven each other in parallel, "If we can't rely on the relics to keep us safe, we can hardly be blamed—"

He stopped abruptly, yelping as he walked into and reversed out of a sharp blackthorn. Clement was looking around her, pointlessly, in the hope that she would somehow be inspired as to where they were and how they might get back onto their track. They had set out to the west, thinking they could simply follow the boundary of the field around and thereby encompass the troops hoping for blessing. But in the dark, with the tracks hidden by hillocks of snow, and their feet slipping out from under them, Clement and Bosco had come away from the ditch, their sole guide, and in returning to it they had veered, they now thought, through one of the gaps into the neighbouring field.

Bosco had seen a light and, eager to get his ordeal over and done with, would not wait for Clement's hesitations, and her turning this way and that to see if she could work out their direction from the stars. But though her astronomy was better than Bosco's, neither of them could make enough sense of it to find a better path.

"Let us go just a little further," he said, "to where the little bush is, and then we will see what we can see."

Heads down against the wind that cut against the sides of

their faces, they stumped and slithered over the uneven ground and the wind picked up when they stopped where Bosco had pointed. It was in fact a fair-sized tree: the land dipped and they had not seen that the light that had guided them was not from their own camp, but that of the aliens.

The enemy army was camped in the centre of the field. At the centre of the camp was a dark red dome, and in concentric rings around it, like the white of an egg around the yolk, were a couple of dozen smaller domes. They glowed only very dimly, as though someone had lit a tiny fire under apricot halves. With the light behind them, the figures moving silently around the domes were in silhouette but their shapes could not be clearly seen. A few feet away, two figures stood, apparently conversing in low voices. One of the figures looked vaguely like a man, apart from having eyes as big as those of a horse and seemingly being made of tubes and pipes from the mouth down. This figure was pale and wore a long tunic, dark but glimmering. The other figure—

Bosco and Clement lived close to the sea, and strange creatures, having died, sometimes washed ashore to be discovered by fisher-folk and sailors. The small ocean-ships that came to their harbours did not travel far, though once when they were very little they had seen a currach with a great sail come ashore with what seemed like a phenomenal number of sailor-men aboard, and extraordinary tales of wild islands and seas of ice. But their home also touched the border of Muinbeo and sometimes ships of an entirely different nature were to be seen; great high-rigged vessels carving a path through the distant stars, or straining in the lightless sky against an invisible anchor. Once they had been playing on the seashore with friends from school, and such a ship had come close to the water. With much shouting and splashing the adults from the village had approached it, wading up to their knees in the sea. The children stayed on the sand, staring in astonished silence at the ship, and at a figure they could see standing at the prow.

It must have been the same species, standing in the snow now, turning towards Clement and Bosco. It looked like it was made from water, sparkling and ruby-coloured, and shifting slowly like a kaleidoscope. Like the violet figure on the prow of the ship years ago, this being seemed hardly to really have a body at all, but to be a set of crystalline shapes; Bosco was reminded of snowflakes, Clement of a nautilus shell. Nonetheless, they could tell that this figure was now turned towards them, now looking at its tubular companion, and back to the children. The big-eyed alien stepped forward, and an electric-blue flush ran up some of its side-tubes as they inflated. It began what was presumably its way of speaking, but what Clement and Bosco—and the soldiers who, alerted by the racket of the goats, were now scampering through the snow after the Commander—heard was music of intense and complex elegance.

The warriors slowed down and stopped, in a line behind the Commander and Mill Thomas. Clement and Bosco were standing ahead, one with her hand over her mouth, the other clutching his hat to his throat. After so long being cold and hungry, and being afraid, and of nothing being important unless it could be eaten or turned into a weapon, to hear something that had no use except this melancholy beauty was overwhelming. To be there when it stopped was heart-breaking. There was absolute silence.

Clement and Bosco regained themselves at the same time. As Bosco's elbow flashed out to nudge her, Clement fumbled with the strap of the harp and pulled it round. Her hands were shaking and tears spilled out of her eyes. Beside she heard an almighty and liquid snort, and saw Bosco wiping his face on his sleeve. Clement racked her brains; the impatient little man who taught her to play the harp always told her that she was the most inattentive brat ever to cross his path. But from the far corners of her mind, she dredged up the best she could do. She rubbed her fingers together to warm them up, and with a couple of hesitant starts, she began to play *Deirdre's Lament*, which, being an Hibernian love-song, had a magnificent desolation.

When she had finished playing, the two aliens made little murmuring noises, and gentle bowings and noddings suggestive of appreciation. The shifting figure, the fluid red spangled with gold in the camp-light, moved forward a few inches, and its billows and drapes fluttered. The sound that it made was soaring and hollow, it sounded like the depths of the sea, like whales, like caverns of ice. When it finished, everyone clapped, but this made the aliens step back in alarm, and several others rush forward, stopping in front of their commanders and taking up crouched positions, with a great many hands held out in defence. Clement looked over her shoulder at the Commander. Mac Cormac said,

"Play *The Night-Jar.*"

Her tone of voice suggested it would go badly with Clement otherwise. The Commander sang dutifully and in tune, if not particularly musically, a cheerful drinking song. When she stopped, all her warriors clapped, and on seeing that this was a good thing, not a threat, the aliens relaxed. On a tide of murmuring, more aliens came forward. It was like, they said later, pictures of the creation of the world, or tales of the Ark, where every species and being had its representative. More horse-eyed figures with their tubes and pipes and air-sacs, more kaleidoscopic cloaks of gold- or pearl-sheened ebony, indigo, ruby and emerald, some bulky shapes that most resembled the undersides of lobsters in glistening amber.

There were a dozen or so of the flame-coloured aliens that had rushed forward in response to the applause. Now that the perceived threat was gone, these figures began to fold in on themselves, retracting their necks and drawing their many limbs and digits back in like a forest of telescopes. Instead of being tall angular figures with plenty of teeth, claws and gleaming scales, they were squat little tubs of beasts, with tuft-like ears, white-rimmed red eyes, tiny paws and genial expressions.

More and more of the army appeared, eyes aloft, tentacles weaving, light-sacs swelling brightly. Bosco stood with his mouth hanging open, finally watching three great figures apparently step out of the blackness of the night; they were chameleons from Alletra, and in their natural state they resembled iguana, but with the vast shadowy eyes that were common on their fiery native planet, long, sharp fingers and opposable thumbs.

These chameleon figures loomed starkly against the orange glow from the aliens' camp, then they vanished and reappeared near the leaders of their own side. They huddled together, only the occasional glittering billow, blood-red gleam of an eye, or some gesturing tentacles being visible to those on the human side. There was matching murmurs and whisperings from the Commander, Mill Thomas and some of the other officers but when the soldiers began to hesitate to continue singing, the Commander strode past with her officers, pausing only to tell Clement to keep playing, and to lift the cumdach from around Bosco's neck.

The huddle of alien officers separated, and they moved— almost flowed—away to one side, the Commander and the officers following. Bosco and Clement looked at each other, and saw their opposites on the alien side begin to falter, looking at each other, and at where the commanders were gathered. Clement cleared her throat, and flexed her fingers till the joints cracked, making Bosco wince.

"Right," she said, "Apparently we have guests to entertain."

The aliens did not seem to notice that Clement had a limited repertoire, but responded to her enthusiasm rather than her skill. From amongst the assembled soldiers, a few more volunteers were sought. A fiddler skipped forward willingly enough, the cook had a bodhrán and the goat-keeper a set of uileann pipes, but two soldiers with tin-whistles were shy enough to have to be dragged forward bodily. Some of the opposing soldiers hurried on their various flippers and feet back to their shelters, and emerged with their own instruments. With the light behind them, it was hard to tell what any of these looked like, apart from one that sounded exactly like a squeeze-box, one that seemed to be all pipes and buttons like an organ, and one that when beaten with a stick sounded like a thousand tiny figures dancing a hornpipe on the ice.

It seemed no time at all when the Commander came back alone. She returned unobtrusively, sidling up past the soldiers playing and clapping and singing, and came to sit beside Clement.

"Good," she said, "If you're tired, give the harp to me."

Clement, whose fingers were tingling painfully, passed over the instrument, and the Commander settled it on her lap. Bosco hissed,

"Where's the cumdach?"

"Be quiet."

"Where's the cumdach?"

"Be quiet. That's an order."

"Where's the cumdach? There'll be mutiny!"

The Commander glowered at him, and began to play a lively and intricate jig, for the other musicians to pick up. Bosco and Clement were the only ones sitting so close to her that they could hear her when she said,

"They proposed—not an alliance, exactly, but a way for both of us to survive a little longer. The invaders have taken over many other worlds, and most of their soldiers are unwelling, many were press-ganged or taken in as slaves. They have no loyalty to our enemy, but we share a fear of their power. We are at a borderland with Over Beyond. With Muinbeo.'

"What has that to do with the cumdach?"

"Not the cumdach but what is inside it. On the Muinbeo side, they are building—re-building—their great fortification at this boundary. The aliens know a way for the Muinbeons to strengthen the fortification, but they need the manuscript. They will bring it back."

Bosco sincerely hoped so. The music went on, and gradually his anxiety left him. Even if the aliens did not bring back the manuscript, it was not his to worry about. It was the Commander who had to keep the army together and either she thought this was the way to do it, or she had a plan in hand if something went wrong. If this was his last hour, at least it was one to remember.

Within the hour the aliens returned. They too kept to the shadows, preferring that their soldiers did not see them, blending in to the back of the crowd; and one, the tubular figure with the glorious voice, appeared at the Commander's side. Hastily shoving the harp at Clement, the Commander stood up, and the alien held out the cumdach. It looked exactly the same, except that in the socket where the moonstone had been, there was now a big oval of some red mineral, gleaming red like the heart of a ruby, with tiny black flecks embedded here and there. The alien touched this, then pointed to the sky, and made a sweeping, protective movement. The Commander looked relieved, and nodded. Bosco hoped this meant that whatever was the red stone, it would help them against the invaders, their common enemy. It could have meant anything.

The music and dancing lasted well into the night, then the officers on either side began to herd their soldiers and animals back to camp. The slowing lights dimmed from the alien side, and Clement and Bosco clambered gratefully into their makeshift beds, the coldness of the straw-lined ground alleviated to some degree by the dog on one side and the goat on the other.

The army slept so late that the sun was bright on the snow by the time Bosco and Clement crawled out of bed and stretched their cramped limbs. Bosco took the cumdach and hung it around his neck. He went to find the Commander.

He found her down by the edge of the field, looking out over the ditch. The blackthorns and brambles were black against the white ground and the milky sky. Here and there a holly shone like an emerald, and bright red berries and late rose-hips were strung along the bare hedgerows. There were even some golden crab-apples not yet fallen from the branches, which were being eaten by the fieldfare.

"Should I walk round the camp?" he asked, "To give the soldiers protection?"

"Against whom should you protect them?" she said, and Bosco looked out over the empty, undisturbed field where the aliens had camped. Bosco took the battle-book from around his neck, and in bewilderment handed it to the Commandant. The red stone was dull and frosted in the morning light.

"We must set off as soon as we have eaten," she said, "We must march to meet the Earl."

The Meaning of Frogs

WHY RED, of all colours, why not white? Yellow? Maybe the dress, lobster-like, had started out as blue but turned red once immersed in the invincible sun. Hot enough to make you put four bullets in a dead man. The sea should be cool, it carried the burden of blue that the veiled sun had scorched out of the dusty sky. There was no reaching it. The water rustled up the shore, sighed as it fell back, a highlight on the distant washing and swashing of the farther sea. The waves did not crash, but ran themselves out over the sand, briefly beautiful in pale lace, then spreading in a glittering pool and being absorbed by the glutted sand. The sand was

> shade would have made all the difference, a hat, even a
> visor, why did she not

The sand was slithering and impossible. Any meaningful sense of direction was gone, one foot stepping though the burning heat and the shifting, replicating sand, no progress, stepping, sinking. Sweating. V felt like some pitiful pack animal condemned to grind corn, and she was only trying to get back to the hotel. Sweat stung her eyes. She could see it spangling her eye-lashes, like a bizarre fashion statement, and mop as she might, the sweat stung and blinded, momentarily fracturing and refracting the shoreline, white and yellow and the line of blue approaching and sighing away. V wiped her face again. She

> sighing at the thought of the forest, it's a great city for
> urban spaces, they know how to live in a city, here, not
> like at home or the Great Wen with everyone crushed
> together

She thought the sea might be coming in, the tide, or it might be going out. Going out, on balance. The sand had a dense, dark band of brown, amber, where the washing waves had soaked it too deeply for even the roasting temperatures of midday to dry out. The sand above the line was glowing white, so bright the shadows were still yellow. It was soft as dust. It was nearly impossible to walk over, neither down to the water and the sparkling waves, nor up, over the billowy slope to where, some-where, there was a hard-track path to the city. Ellie had suggested a walk in the woods but

could have, maybe should have, gone to the forest, the woods, that had been Ellie's suggestion, go in among the trees instead of down to the sea, yes? No? Maybe? On balance, V had said, no, she needed to get her head in the game for the afternoon sessions. If she had said yes, then

then the shaded leaves would be cool, tacky to the touch maybe, the upper side glaubous and shining. The ground would be cool too, mulched with low plants in dark rosettes, no dust.

but the *no* created *this*, the yielding, tormenting sand, the unreachable sea, and the blazing helmet of an achromatic sky. The *yes* would have yielded the forest, and it would be full, surely, polyphonic ringing of chirrups and trills, and not the furious, desolate ululation of a sea-bird. The sea rolled, thrumming like an engine, and the birds shrieked, and V mopped silently, and plodded on. Even Sisyphus got to the top of the mountain, meaningless as the arrival might have been, but at least not like this stupid struggle, the practice of pointlessness that was this dry wading through

no wind to speak of, though faint scorchings, as though

from a secretive opening of a distant furnace door

A dust-devil? In the distance?

Hardly. Is that even what they are called? No. V couldn't remember. There were many things she could not remember. Was *glaubous* even a word? There had not been a single word spoken at the conference so far that would have driven her to a dictionary. That was a thought that gave her comfort. More sand slopped over her feet, and she nearly lost her balance. It was not a dust-devil, it was animal, not meteorological. The heat-haze

the sweat in her eyes, too

blurred the shape at first, could have been anything, a seal, a small child. Wild, silent bounding brought whatever it was closer, and the haze and the blur resolved themselves and it was very clearly a dog, and again closer it resolved itself further into the specificity of a yellow one, a Labrador, young, and long-legged, with a slash of muscular pink lolling out of its mouth like an arm out of a car window.

Sand was flying up and vanishing in the beating glare of the sun while a dog-tangle of limbs scampered up-slope. And the target now revealed, a gang of seagulls, six, or nine, stretching their necks and their membranous yellow hooks. V stopped abruptly to squint, shading her eyes, her feet slipping. The birds bolted up into the air, shooting away from the explosion of dog, countering the rapid barking with their own wailing calls. Three black crows hopped, and lifted up a couple of feet into the pale air, and landed quickly, bouncing a little on the sand like balls rolling towards entropy. The yellow dog trotted back to the seashore with an air of profound delight, and trotted briskly in the shallow water that ran up to obliterate its tracks.

V patted her head cautiously, testing

> sunstroke heat stroke dehydration wet kerchief on the
> neck the hat lying on the hotel armchair

> testing how high above her

crisping hair she could feel the aureole of heat. Turning down
Ellie's invitation—what great teeth these people had, really,
sterling choppers altogether—V had believed her own voice,
and its talk of getting her head in the game for the afternoon
sessions, and wanting to think over the presentations of
yesterday—

> reflection on, planning for: fairy-tales, in this heat—dry
> and uncooperative as the sand, bullying, insistent sand,
> overly compliant with the stepping foot, but tricksy,
> unreliable. Trying to inch up the slight sandy slope city-
> wards was the stuff of despair. Sand trickled inexorably
> into her shoes and stung her searing feet

The sun was so dazzling that the small group of people with
their yoga mats and their bottles of water appeared to manifest
from thin air. Whoever was leading them wore very pale purple
clothes, very shining, rippling, very loose, they could have
vanished against the farther water. V stopped to watch them.
She had not expected to see anyone doing this, but she knew
that it was a regular occurrence, tai chi on the beach. She ran
her hands stickily through her sweating hair, and by the grace
of the gods there was a tiny breath of breeze that cooled her
damp scalp. The tai chi was just starting. The group stood very
tall with their faces raised, like sunflowers. One of them wore
white. They started to move, slowly stepping, and turning,
crouching, smoothing the air with their open hands, stretching
out, recoiling with infinite grace. V recalled

> a very long time ago, though, now—not that flexible.
> Send me back and have me re-assembled before I could
> do that standing on one leg lark.

V recalled that every move-
ment was a movement into or out of a form that had to be
achieved. White Crane, Golden Rooster, Wild Horse. The
group was expert and serene, and they glided, arching their
wrists and bunching their fingers together as though lifting a
sodden something, describing an arc by skimming each thigh
in succession along the burning sand, changing direction,
without advancement; V inched down towards the water

hammering the harder sand near the
water and walkers scattering like alarmed birds—horses. They
were horses. Six or nine of them. In the haze, they seemed quite
far away, all dark, nearly blue, dark blue against the intense
bright-ness of the sand, the dazzling colourlessness of the air.
V stopped and mopped and squinted. The haze

occasionally wanted to be a horse but no significant
longing to own one though loved those holidays with
them, even ponies

The haze, the
dusty sunshine, settled or cleared and the horses were very
quickly extremely close, glossy and dark and very, very close,
hooves drumming like impatient fingers, no sign of riders but
the sun was so blinding that shrivelled eyeballs could be persuaded of anything the horses and their blue fracturing forms
and their thrumming like wasps wild in the heart of an apple
and everyone spattering hastily up the sand to sanctuary.

V staggering as best she could out of the way—
slipping back again   again   into her own disappearing
footprints   first faint flickering of frantic   of panic   of
hunted hounded
The horses had passed by, streaming horsehair.
V turned, her feet grinding and slipping, to watch the horses
undulate up the beach. Turning her back on the sun afforded
her, unexpectedly, a modicum of relief from squinting the

brightness out of her eyes. She mopped her face once more, and it remained dry. *Remember Columbae*, she thought unexpectedly, *on former shifting sands when wind blew unknown treasures in their faces*. She could not remember the name of the poet. *Secrets waiting in Elysian fields*. A school poem? Maybe. She could not remember. V looked down at the sand as an excuse to an indifferent but judgemental world for resting a few moments longer. The sand was churned about where the yellow Labrador dog had scattered, as joyfully as a pile of copper and ruby leaves, the birds. Behind her, out over the sea, the seagulls were circling and calling, like bells they rang, wheeling, and changing their cries, from the long wails of loss and fear to short, fat-throated calls to plenty.

A frog lay in one of the yellow hollows.

The frog was still glistening. It lay on its side, one hind leg extended as though it was being pinned out for dissection, and the rest of its body twisted, turning its underside modestly away from view. V got down on her hunkers and contemplated the corpse. The frog's olive-brown body was about two inches long, meaning, she forced herself to calculate, that when alive, it could have jumped nearly twelve feet easily. A frog jumping was the closest thing she could imagine to the instantaneous move from one place to another that was possible only by mythical beings. She remembered these movements: the frog hunched, and the briefest flicker of shadow and green, and the frog was elsewhere. V stretched out her hand and touched the stretched leg. The underside of the corpse was pale, buttery yellow. There was not the slightest movement. She kept her finger out, and touched the cream hollow where the thigh joined the torso. It was dead, naturally.

The seizure of the frog by seagull or crow or whatever it might have been had ripped up its belly, before losing it to the sand. The frog's inside was bright and perfect, and perfectly wrong, being turned onto the outside. V prodded the guts tentatively. Her nail dented some soft tissue and the light slid over the tiny edge. She couldn't tell one organ from another, but they were brightly coloured and shining, as hard and clear a reflection of the sun as if they were made out of plastic, still as neatly tucked into their places as a flat-packed table un-packed, wound around each other, nestling.

In any event, the frog was dead, and V's knees were beginning to ache. The splayed attitude of the frog invited a form of pity, though not the thought of predator and prey. The position, unthinkably vulnerable in the living, was an announcement of the death, the endedness of the life. Perhaps it was the waste that touched her—if the frog was not dinner, it may as well have lived. It looked thwarted in its twisted aspect, an ultimate sacrifice discarded. To be alive, and be dead, be eaten, were not injustices, but Ellie had suggested a walk in the woods but—dismissed. Thinking

the ruthlessness of the inescapable Moirae was not as terrible as unkindness and disregard

Thinking neither yes nor

no, without reflecting or assessing, V picked up the dead frog. It was so light it barely pressed her skin, hardly firmly enough to transfer damp, or grains of sand. When she cupped her hand, the frog turned or was turned over. Even dead, its skin was like emerald, amber, and it still shone

and glasses cracking together like breaking

bones, ice rattling, laughter, like sea-swells, currents, but without rhythm, and raucous, and pitched too

glaucous, dammit, not glaubous. Christ. Is glaubous even a word? Glaucous is the wrong one, anyway, meaning grey, from Latin, from Greek, meaning bloomy

and pitched too high. The hotel

foyer rang with voices. V took the glass that sterling-toothed

Ellie gave to her, and raised it just far enough to be sociable. She was firmly repelled by the thought of drinking any of the gummy-looking red, orange-red, liquid it contained. At the same time, she knew the rules, especially the unspoken ones. She drew in a deep breath, into her diaphragm, and breathed out slowly. These events were always much the same. Once the steps

> jive and lindy-hop quadrille, reel and hornpipe and ch-ch-
> ch-ch-cha-cha

> Once

the steps were known they could be performed with both serenity

> god give me the serenity to accept the things I cannot

serenity and grace. Even *with* a dead frog up her sleeve. She pictured the high steppings and the glidings of the figures on the beach. She didn't even have to stand on one leg. All she had to do was concentrate.

Ellie was drinking something bright yellow. The rim of her glass was crusted with salt, or sugar. Someone, one of the afternoon's presenters, pushed by, jostling V. They turned, touched her shoulder, and apologized, smiling at Ellie.

"Good point, yes, interesting idea you made," he said to V, "You thought so too, no, Ellie? About moving the company's Executives Park further away. But you know, you shouldn't believe everything those protesters say, those, you know, activists. They have their heads in the clouds, don't know the real world."

V made the pretence of taking a mouthful of drink, thinking quickly, her mind immediately alert to consequences.

> Bird on a current   Migratory   detecting magnetic fields
> and plunging into the wind

He was leaning far too close to V's ear, his voice cracking a little with the strain of being heard, looking at Ellie as he spoke.

The walk back from the sea shore, hurried, late, but at least not struggling on the shifting, tricksy sand canal   a strip of amber or of toffee green boa on each side and the white apartment buildings reflected   right at the end the protestors singing and eating ice-cream

"I suppose, though," said Ellie, trying to balance on an uncertain fence, "We are supposed to take the, you know, environmental issues into consideration."

"We have to take our clients into consideration," the man corrected her, and she laughed accordingly. "No, yeah, it's all very well to claim the Executive Park will do whatever—cut across the," a wave of the hand while he plucked words wildly from the air, "the migratory paths of bloody puffins or what- ever it is," and he smiled at Ellie laughing again, "but you can't save the panda by shooting the Chinese."

He nodded with finality, and strode off firmly.

"...eally great, wasn't it"

Ellie's voice was too thin to be clearly heard, so V nodded, *mmm, mmmm*. Ellie seized her arm, and leaned in a fraction.

"Are you okay?"

She narrowed her eyes as though she was puzzled, and shifted them swiftly side to side, looking into each one of V's eyes separately, as mediocre actors do to convey intensity.

"A touch of the sun," V said wildly, impulsively. Ellie looked instantly concerned. V's spirits plunged. Sisyphus again. Ellie would not be making such an effort had she not been convinced that by V's age, she would be far higher up the corporate ladder, rebuilding whole cities, not just devising plans for an Executive Park, however controversial, for one global client. V felt a wild, wild impulse to tell Ellie not to bother, that she didn't have V's stamina, that sharks have even better teeth, second sets, even. But officially Ellie was her intern, so officially, V had to believe in her abilities, and her chances. Ellie was saying something else, but the noise was too loud. There were random phrases everywhere, like confetti, erratic gouts of sound, like a radio with a spinning dial.

> *...sort of man to really throw a rope around this project...*
> *...ike the 'screw it, let's do it' attitude you get at home but you just...*
> *...genuinely transformative ideas about pathways to...*
> *...eal paradigm-shifting thinking...*

Perhaps she did have a touch of the sun

    setting in a last blaze, a burning weal in a mild sky rose mackerel clouds still warm but cool and even a breath of breeze

The French windows on the east side of the hotel opened out into a small, cobbled courtyard. The sun was too low to touch the immaculate planters and the few raised flowerbeds, but the polished metal and the varnished wood had an incarnadine glow, set off by the dark, charcoal shadows. The hotel was in a quiet part of the city, between the ambassadorial residences and the Old Town, a wealthy part, where people had gardens with songbirds in them, and where the washing of the tide was sometimes carried on the wind. Someone stepped out through the doors, behind V, and made some remark about the relief from the disorienting sun of the day. V hastily tucked the frog back into her sleeve. She could hardly ask a complete stranger to act as chief mourner while V put the frog to rest on a plant-er. They made desultory, peaceful conversation, and then her companion said, very quickly, almost conspiratorially,

"We have been trying for some time to encourage your employer to consider the environmental impact."

"They think it isn't the real world."

"I would like—if you would like to take—"

The proffered business card was of a subdued colour, and the light from the reception only just sufficient for V to read that the holder was from the municipal offices.

Accept or decline, yes or no, no or yes.

V was not sure how long she had hesitated before she took the card. What was too long to

no or yes, no to the no, yes, yes

to accept? She was losing her sense of consequences.

Her correspondent gave a brief, but intensely delighted, puff of laughter. The wind had changed quarters, and the washing of tide was both hypnotic and soporific

the water over her face was very blue, very bright. The light was very yellow. V wondered if something had been added to the water to make it look so definitely blue like topaz or aquamarine. She repeated the words, blowing bubbles. Topaz. Aquamarine. Bubbles. The strong yellow of the light.

how many years since the last occasion for using topaz in a sentence? Gamboge! There's a thought

The bath was long enough to lie down in. The last hotel she had stayed in, the bath was so small it was more like a girdle. Less and less allotted space.

girdle, bubble, bubble, corset

V sat up.

The frog was in the emptied pot-pourri bowl, emptied of scented fragments of wood, and refilled with ice blagged from the hotel bar. Not exactly blagged. Some expansive whiskey-soured executive at the reception, standing between V and one of the interns, gripping one shoulder in each squashy, warm palm, saying *well ladies?* Shamelessly V waved at someone, and abandoned her accidental companion, sending someone from HR over to keep an eye on things, slipping out of the range of each stretched hand, saying *I must just talk to…* and *I'm afraid Gilbert is looking for me!* knowing that no-one would have the chutzpah to say *Who the fuck is Gilbert?* Or worse again, *I'm Gilbert, who the fuck are you?* She had gone to the bar, asked for a large glass of ice, and as the barman filled a pint glass with chunks of ice, V asked impulsively for a small glass of wine. She was handed a third of a bottle in a glass the size of her head. Internally, she shrugged with a feeling of reprieve—*well, I* asked *for a small one.* The bath was perfect.

The forest might have been perfect. Cool, anyway. Why had she said no?

her own voice, saying brightly, …*got to get my head in the game for this afternoon's*

What kind of a phrase was that? Get my head in the game? Head in the noose more like

it used to be believed that a bear had to lick its formless cub into the proper shape—that was what *yes* and *no* did, this *yes* and that *no* led to this life; reversed, everything would have been different—

Sisyphus and Kassandra, arm in arm, the whole bleak cycle of meaninglessness churning away like sand under running feet

Perhaps she had really had a touch of the sun—the phrase stood out, having a hieratic ring to it. A euphemism for sacrifice. *Where's Wally? Oh…he had a touch of the sun. Mithras ate him.* V took a mouthful of blood-red wine. She slid down under the water again.

Only when the water had become chilly did she get out of the bath. The towel was disappointing. It was enormous but did not absorb moisture properly, and was too soft to warm the skin through rubbing. V used the previous day's shirt instead. The whole room had a manipulative air, appearing to offer great comfort—armchair, table, dressing table, as well as two beds—but being in fact extremely cramped, because everything was so finely measured that nothing could be moved into a more useable position. V ordered a meal to be delivered, and sat on the bed to watch the awkwardly placed television. Miraculously, there was a film on that she knew she was just tipsy enough to enjoy. Normally, there were double bills of *The Simpsons* and then an over-acted, under-written film based on someone's true story.

V was woken by the fire-door slamming. Her waking jerk spilled a little wine from the glass tilting in her hand, and she had a stabbing crick in her neck from having fallen asleep slumping. The film was coming to an end, the fashion designer making her protest by having all her catwalk models naked, and outside, voices were ringing down the corridor. V's heart was thumping in her throat. She set the glass down sharply, and untangled herself from the slithering duvet. The spyhole in the door allowed only a limited view, and that warped, but the source of the racket was clear enough. The reception had ended and debouched the tipsy onto their routes to bed. Some of them were standing around talking loudly. Others were striding away, their hard heels striking the synthetic carpet so vigorously that sparks should have flown. Peals of laughter. Someone's children, newly woken and already primed with over-excitement and too much sugar, started racing up and down. Their banshee wailing was undented by a voice, presumably their parent's, saying mildly, *Shush! Not so much noise!* More peals of laughter.

V tiptoed away from the door. Under cover of the noise outside, she made a mug of tea, staring at the frog in its ice-bath, neither seeing it nor blinking. She stood at some random point in the room, and listened to the annoying voices and the braying laughter. Her consciousness of the physical distance between her and her colleagues, and of her absolute absence from their consciousness, was so profound that she felt like she had acquired a new sense or revitalized a vestigial one.

Eventually, the sounds died away. The children were wrangled into their beds, and even their unpredictable cries of protest were absorbed by closing doors, and firm voices. The footsteps found their bedrooms, fumbled with their keys. V opened the window as far as it would go, and listened for the sea. The wind had changed its quarter again, and it was the sound of the city at night that she heard, clear and hard as blades.

the inescapable feeling of having escaped though not
pursued   the potential, though, anyone else up early
breakfasting   not unreasonable to take the longer road
to the sea   there's a thought   it was the same canal as
yesterday   green reedy beard the coolness after all that
sun   the people singing
oh and the sea reaching up
and so *much* further,   waves further up too, proper
crashing, not the approach and washing retreat of
yesterday   not a bit of it   the thin shrill spilling   good
solid heaving and collapsing   far by the horizon all that
blue dark dusty wide sea bloomy blue and wide reach of
sky run together   the sun lurking lazily behind that
opalescence that'll soon burn off but now   the

The blurred percussion of the sea withdrawing the tide made a lively accompaniment to the solo calling of the seabirds, coasting at wild angles on the wind currents, and modelled in slashes of bright white and glossy black against hazy mauve sky. The wind, naturally, was higher too, but not so high as to be unpleasant or to blow the sand about discouragingly. V wore both a hat and a light jacket. The band of wet sand below the high tide mark was wide enough to walk upon with ease, and she stopped now and then, to look out at the foam and the slatey troughs. She swung her arms out, and strode.

There were people on the beach, but not many. They were mostly out with their dogs. Some of the dogs were flinging themselves into the laundering water, eyes rolling, some were content to hang back until the wave ran out, and then to run into the few inches that were left. Some of the humans were stumping along resignedly, a disposable cup of some refreshment in one hand, extending their tongues like frogs' to trap the flaccid croissant or *croque monsieur* that they held in the other. Others walked in pairs, intently talking. A few ran in and out with the dogs, flinging tennis-balls or sticks.

Up on the high bank of sand and marram grass, two other figures were lying with a stealthy air about them. They lay on their fronts, an adult and a child, parallel streaks of rusty brown, pale hats tipped back. The adult turned its head, evidently spoke to the child, who turned in its turn to reply. V could just see the object of their attention: a white cow, a Highland from the horn-tips visible, and lying down in the grass. She glimpsed it through a gap in the grass as she passed. It was curled up, resting, chewing, its hair the same bleached beige as the sand, but the shadows making its rump orange.

V strode on, sometimes swinging her arms, stopping to feel the breeze, or to admire the full-throated, plump-breasted loveliness of it all. She was headed for the groyne, the first and longest of three, and the one that made a narrow pathway out into the sea. The sea was battering around the edges but was not high enough to splash over the top.

The city did not encourage people to walk along the groyne but of course they did it, it was a magnet for photographers, for children seeking yet another way to scare the shit out of their parents, for courting couples, and now for someone seeking a suitable graveyard for a dead frog. V clambered up onto the groyne. It was easily done. The wind was marginally higher and the cobbled surface slightly slippy. V walked to the end of the groyne, and took out of her pocket the corpse of the frog.

Waves flicked their white tops over the cobbles. To her left, there was a still patch in the bright water, a quieter area with a discolouration but not many waves. She wondered if that was pollution, and thought grimly of the reluctant dog-walkers with their disposable cups. She turned her gaze back to the clearer water.

On her way to the beach, she had plucked a couple of dock-leaves, and used these as a shroud, knotting the stalks together. She was torn between feeling vaguely as though there ought to be some form of ritual, and feeling vaguely silly that she had the thought. In the end, she muttered *better luck next time, acushla,* and used both hands to throw the frog out to sea. It came loose of the dock leaves, which were instantly whipped away by the wind, and blown north, while the frog described a perfect arc through the air. It was a tiny fleck on the blue of the sky, the mauve, the darker blue, grape-dark, of the deeper sea, and its limbs were splayed, like a cog, V thought first, and dismissed the thought, there was too much joyousness in the frog's spinning parabola. It disappeared into the water.

V, in her turn, slipped on the wet cobbles, and fell back like a plank into the shockingly deep sea.

For the first foot it looks so bright like turquoise and emerald like it has soaked all the blue from the sky—

immersed immediately in cold and heaviness   cold enough to stop your blood in its tracks   there is no grasping it   the few seconds of water rustling into ears and eyes then absolute silence

water is slithering and impossible, unnegotiable   not

> even sense of direction except face up, face down, one
> arm striking out to galvanize the body into a swimming
> action, a foot kicking   freezing   every inch of water
> replicating   water veiling her eyes   forcing them open
> water rolling

V came to the surface, turned over, and went under again.

> *rip-tide* sandy water pushing out *undertow* speeding under
> pressure out to sea
> swim parallel no meaningful sense of direction all gone
> like the air
> parallel to shore and kicking, striking against the
> slithering, yielding, bullying water

V came to the surface again. She was far from shore, but could still strike out for the groyne. The world was fractured to bits through the sea streaming through her hair but she did not go under again, nor was she being bowled out to sea. She began to swim but without any real sense of how to make her limbs function as swimming tools, she kicked convulsively, splashing and flailing her arms, spitting and gasping. She jammed her foot against the base of the groyne and experiencing a pain far more intense than the fear. It concentrated her mind on the ground, rocks, not the water. Barefoot and sodden, and in a state of crippling uncertainty, she clambered out of the water and onto the knobbly groyne.

> sit tight, and not back in the water. Yes to the solid
> ground, no to the water.

She should have known, she used to know, about riptides. She had been warned about them often enough. One of her earliest memories, one that was the rarest recollections among her rare recollections, was of splashing out into the sea at the age of about three, paddling in the ripples between plates of smooth water, walking, kicking joyfully out to where the water was foamy and discoloured, and her father's brother, racing towards her. She registered the open mouth but not the shouting. He grabbed her and whirled her out of the water and then, unused to children, still shaken, and afraid that he had frightened her, he explained riptides.

Had he been slower. Had she gone farther. And again, now.

had the riptide not been losing power   had I been caught
          in the middle   had I not been able to get away cold
        enough to stop the blood in your veins   so dark it had
      soaked all the blue from the sky   the slightest difference
                the slightest clapping of a butterfly's wing and
      drowning's a terrible way to go though   of all choices, the
        toughest   fill your pockets with stones and walk into the
      Thames   but this   a mindless yes or no an unconcerned
            the frog had died and frogs go on   it had a function
            beyond its practice of everyday   Ellie and the other
    interns   Sisyphus and Kassandra   the heat-death of the
                                                          universe

V cleared the sea from her eyes

                      alive dead sunsets puffins cat's eye nebulae
        the hair's-breadth, absolute hair's breadth, binary, riptide
    calm water, dead alive, safe endangered, yes no yes

Thicker Than Blood

WHOEVER HAD a name to match their destiny? I thought of changing mine—to Fionnuala, perhaps, keening on the shores on Moyle, or Helen, stolen away like a robbed parcel. But it could, I realized, have been worse and at least I was called after a legendary sea-wave. So Cliona I have remained and the aquatic life in which I found myself thrust I have now embraced. Like earth and ocean I was born in violence, the physical form through the violence of an undrugged childbirth, my vampiric self through the violence of my sire's unreflective lust. When the cooling of the universe brought electrons and protons together, expanses of time was needed for the adhesion of matter, the genesis of hydrogen and oxygen. Loss of heat and an ocean of time; without these things life could never have come about. Loss of blood-heat, and in the atto-time vampires inhabit, I have become something extraordinary.

Having died in the water, I awoke in the water, and it has become my protection from the sun. I can recall the last time I feared water, I can recall the very evening, when my brother, his thirst for blood sated, flung my dying body into Galway Bay. When I first moved to the underwater, I lived virtually alone and liked it. I was neither human nor demon, dead nor alive, so I might as well, I thought, be neither alone or in company. When I first left the land, Gráinne Mhaol was still on the high seas, and when I re-emerged, the acephalous ruins of the Federated Empire and the syphilitic descendants of the Empire's former neophytes were labouring in the pit, each blindly dedicated to the comminution of the other. The justification for the war was the rhetoric of an enclosed metaphysics, but the execution of it had at first a terrifying grandeur.

Now they have just become two boxers whose fists graft

themselves to the other's face at each blow and must be torn asunder till finally every organ is exposed and dry and the last synapse has flickered out. Every conceivable form of energy has been exhausted, even prisoners of war on tread-mills the size of countries. Humans had even begun looking to the uncolonized planets, hoping insanely for refuge from insanity under the sulphur rains and on the boiling rocks of Venus. Since I have recognized that life in general, and my life in particular, cannot exist without water, I have felt better, knowing that I had retained some connexion with the mortals.

But now the connexion is drawing closer because the mortals are stepping silently to shores across Europe and the Americas, as they were known, and, with a last cautious glance, slipping under the water. So I am not travelling all these thousands of miles back to the scene of my desanguination just for merriment. Now that the humans, whom I once forcibly left, have come to my world, there is a job to do. There is nothing left now but the electricity generated by buckyballs.

The possibility of re-infecting myself with an emotional attachment to the place of my birth had not occurred to me, and it is some time before I realize the real reason that I spend the night walking the shores of Inis Mór, not the mainland. For two centuries I saw no humans unless I sought them out, then in the twentieth century humans began to investigate the oceans. At first—my sense of humour having been drained from my veins along with my blood—I shunned them, preferring to hide in caves and remind myself of how full of sour grapes and ashes was my life. By and by I began to watch them, fascinated by the machines they brought with them, in their way imitations of biology. Ships glided over my head, over the centuries, dropping sounding bells and sinkers, trying as best they could to create a map of the ocean floor.

I hid in the sonar shadows, marvelling at all that the mortals missed. Occasionally, I admit, I teased them; as my body adapted to allow me to live in the ocean, I let them catch glimpses of me as I sped away leaving a trail of light behind me. After a century or two, I never thought of my past. But when I reach the edge of Ireland's continental shelf I dream a dream I have not had in many years, and when I wake I know I have been crying. My tears are dense globes, sinking slowly through the salt water; I dreamed I could breathe again. A winter breath it was, when the veins of ice in the air crawl, crackling in the mouth, roughening the throat, stretching the warm lungs till they smart and flush. Then out. Great lungfuls of pure air, right from the open atmosphere, standing right up on a mountain side in the sunlight, with no protective mile of water above me.

When I awoke I was still so thrilling with the feel of air in my body that desolation swamped my waking self. This dream has always made me sad, reminding me of what I have lost. But now, with humans barely able to breathe the air either, I weep for all of us. Treasure each breath, it may be your last. It is now, more surely than from the stars upon which I depend, that I know I am almost reached my destination. As I swim towards Inis Mór I slip under a boat, and the bright light I can see from my safe shadows below show me movement, a girl, playing with the clean water. Sound travels more slowly through water than does light so it is moments before I hear her pulse. I flip over and dive. I am *jealous* but I only realize it after circling the rocky island during the night. My emotions are so limited now, that I am sad long before I know what to call it. It is the last moments before dawn when I leave the oceanside. The moon is a fading scar, the horizon has that tremulous violet that is the last passage of the night. I slip into the water, safe from the sun. I no longer need air. I cannot bear light. I am outside time. I am made of earth held falsely together, waiting for a pointed stick to prise them apart. At least I still have water.

Eoghan will certainly be surprised. The little bastard.

Eoghan has always been very clever indeed. He concealed the fact that he is a vampire, having lost his humanity along with his virginity to the strong-thighed daughter of a Carraroe fisherman; he staked her the next time he saw her. He took over our father's merchant livelihood and feigned an illness that allowed him to avoid daylight. Physicians were a problem, as they were for King Midas, and the solution reached in much the same way. As the centuries passed and language developed a specialization for every facet of existence, he became a photophobe. But transparent though his hands might virtually be, they never lost their surety of touch in business and Eoghan remains one of the richest men in Europe by dint of canny selling to all sides. While I am waiting for the sun to go down, I swim to Tor Bucky. It is many miles down, but the obscene skeleton it makes is visible, I would guess, almost from the surface.

The first pipes and bridges were things of ethereal beauty, I remember seeing images of them projected by the news channels onto the night sky. Timeless bones of steel and glass, rising from the land like mermaids, arching between sky and land like something from Plato, the crater snug in the centre like Atlantis. Oceanographers had known about the crater for over a century, and had long speculated that it had been the result of a meteorite crash, but it was nothing more than an oddity until a geologist and an oceanographer were chatting at a party and the one mentioned to the other the high instance of buckyballs in the crater at Sudbury Plain. The oceanographer took herself off to the floor of the Atlantic three miles from the coast, and a year later told the world that the Connemara crater was hopping with buckminsterfullerenes.

Isn't that grand, said Eoghan, bringing forth the Forte family's claim to a big chunk of the sea and all that came out of it—wangled so that the proto-Eoghans could control first the docking of ships, vulture rights to shipwrecks, and fishing, but now a more stable molecule. He had no idea what to do with the discovery and instantly went into partnership with a nanotechnology research company based in the Inca Empire but controlled by an uneasy alliance of businessmen and criminals from across the globe, Red River to Siberia.

Buckyballs and carbon tubes became the commonplace headlines of the *Galway Herald* and the *Carraroe Tribune*. Newspapers included animated images to show the changes in colour with doping but nothing about the experiments my brother was facilitating to investigate the commercial production of electricity by pushing water through buckytubes on an industrial scale. Clean electricity, they said, using the most stable molecule, our companion from the beginning of the world, and with the thickening of the air with pollutants, everyone eagerly said yes.

The research began in earnest and when another century had passed and Eoghan was pretending to be another generation of our family, the first building began on the floor of the Atlantic ocean. A chaotic metal whose molecules did not affect the tiny fullerenes provided the protective shell inside which an intricate network of carbon nanotubes were constantly assailed by the sea and, obedient to their chemical laws, they produced electricity which, unlike power derived from ocean storms, could be generated at will and without stop. And then of course the war had started, and the fighter ships that tore up the sky needed so much fuel that the earth was torn up in its turn to supply it. Like a bear whose bile is in demand, the land has its scars ruptured almost daily so that both the Federated Empires and the Union of Civil Democracies can keep their spybots in the air.

Time passed and Eoghan became greedy; time passed some more and the enemies became more desperate. The earth was ripped and shattered as a car crash, war and greed and mortals piled on top of the earth like a lamprey, and sucked up oil and the fossils fuels like a vampire sucks blood. The sky from Connemara to as far as the eye could see across the Atlantic was a dead red, streaks of sick green marking the clouds of nitrogen. The transport bridges were no longer glass but low-grade unstable metals that scraped the sky like infected cuts. The pipes no longer rose from the ground and blended with the landscape; ditches had been gouged and the pipes laid as best they could fit; with no money spared to pay engineers, the ditches were never deep enough and so lay like cicatrices across the grey land. In some places the ditches were so tight that the pipes were stove in to fit. In other places, the ditches were too big, gaping like hand-me-down shoes, filled with the corpses of fish, drowned dogs, and derelict humans.

Soon the water that had been dragged in to copulate with the buckyballs to produce electricity before being washed out again began to leak from the damaged pipes. The toxicity of industrial scale use of fullerenes laid waste to the land. The bleached earth and mutant animals might never have been my concern except that by the time it showed up on the land, it had already begun to poison my world.

It always pleased me to watch a country build up under the sea. When I was a very young child I used to try to imagine the underside of a country, all those miles below sea-level until it joined the earth. Did every bit of it join up, I asked my father, who looked astonished, or might it break off? Would the eternal ocean, biding its time, wear away the joins, casting islands and continents so adrift that they might some day disappear or bump together? My father, believing as he must in the literal truth of the Bible, looked sternly at my mother who was obliged to reprove me for my curiosity. Since then it has been a comfort to me to see for myself the monolithic roots of a place, a massy link between the world that lies under the sun and that which lies under the water.

My water world is not so protected that I cannot sense the shadow of the mortal world's activities. In 1912 I had been swimming on the cold horizon of the northern oceans when a ship hit an iceberg and plummeted to its doom. I was far too many miles away to see it, and only heard a faint boom hours later, but I knew something had happened. The deep ocean changed the quality of its silence, phosphorescence dimmed instantly, even the whales stopped. We were like birds and gophers when a hawk flies over.

I swim to the edge of Hibernia, and investigate the remainder of its continental shelf, that anchor of my childish imagination and as I swim inland, I glide again under the boat, and find that having been plunged first into *sorrow*, *empathy* and then *jealousy*, I crash into one more clot of vestigial humanity.

How do I put this politely? Eoghan vampirized me while I was out under Spanish Arch, dressed in men's clothes, engaged in my nightly squiring of Hannah Lynch, another merchant's daughter. I am not sure what my mother or her circle would have done with an ichthyic vampire for a daughter, especially one who preferred girls. What I am trying to bring myself to say is that, devastated though I was when Hannah spurned me—not having expected the ichthyic, the vampire or even, I confess, the daughter—and sad though I was when Hannah finally died, I have not lived the life of an anchorite since then. Before I came home to the water I lived much as Eoghan did, though elsewhere, shunning the light, and sulkily coming out at night, in male attire.

Later, of course, when the nanotubes had altered my physiology, and my expedited evolution obediently worked out the evolutionary advantage, it was a little more difficult. I favoured prostitutes as they were not in a position to complain about preferences for being fully clothed, the unexpectedly exposed patch of scaled skin, the occasional gelatinous touch and a tendency to light up at moments of passion—I was clean and I paid. The more treacherous the human world becomes, the more reluctant I am to take on that disguise and that really has only left one option—as I do draw the line at bestiality, however attractive the whale—of myself and my fins.

But looking at the draped limbs and the silver drops thrown up from her casually kicking foot, I wanted nothing more than to shed my new skin and step, finless, lightless, naked as the girl herself, into the little bobbing boat. Foolishly, cautiously I approach the boat and am astonished that she almost immediately rises on her elbow, twitching her head to listen. Humans never see me and almost never sense me. I am not, of course, truly invisible. Animals see me and react to my presence, agitation spasming their skin like electricity, fish and certain plants are instantly elsewhere, in the same nanosecond that they register my trick of silver light. Almost from the first moment I rose choking from Galway Bay, humans became irrelevant to me, like a light switched off. It was many years later, when I realized that I am what I have always been but just in a different combination of flesh, that I also realized that the light switch had been on their side. I was no more than a flit through an open doorway. I dove down till I could not hear her.

The shore of Galway Bay is evening warm under my bare feet, and I stand for a moment at that place I love, the exact spot where the sea and the land meet and part, the exact spot where the sea, with its terrible eternity, will absorb the land, and the land will become the sea. Due to Eoghan's diligence, however, there is little charm to be had here, at the sandy edge of the Atlantic, for he has shattered the land with the architecture needed to bring the electricity from the ocean to the Federation Air Base in the centre of the city—and to surreptitiously siphon some of it away to the Union's Air Base in Reykjavík. Good old Eoghan, sticking firmly by the family's advantageous interpretation of political neutrality. I sigh, and step out towards the house where I was born.

Eoghan is too old to be surprised. Even if he felt the shock of discovering that the young man he had vampirized under Spanish Arch a millennium ago was in fact his sister, his face, encrusted with age and greed and loneliness, could not show it.

"And how is it you think you know this?" he says wearily. There has been a campaign against the use of nanotechnology to support the war, against the use of buckyballs, in favour of discovering the consequences before taking action—the last one almost a human taboo, it seems to me.

"How is it that you think you can prove this?"

He uses our father's study as his office. The walls are still lined with bookshelves, none of which my father or Eoghan ever read. The rise in acid in the air is slowly eating away the leather covers, and leaving bleached streaks on the oak shelves. The floor has had to be replaced with concrete to save Eoghan from falling through the skeletal floorboards, and the windows, enlarged in the 1920's, have been coated to protect him from the sun so the light in the room has a glowing quality, as though it were made of neon, with a definite tinge of violet. Forte House was made of local stone, built on the corpse of a Norman tower, and was altered only when the comfort or safety of my brother required it, so the kitchen, where there are only his servants to work, is the same cold block of sixteenth-century rudiments, while his sitting room has every luxury and protection this century can offer to the rich.

I told him about the corpse I had found, floating off the coast of Greece. He had been a male human, he had been dead a while, but there was enough of him left for me to be astonished—the first human I had ever seen who had done what I had done. I began looking for them, then, the humans who were trying to save themselves from the war and from the hostility of the overground by altering their genetic coding so that they could live underwater. These humans lived closer to the shores of what had been their civilization so they were the first to be affected by the surge in concentration of water-borne fullerenes. It was other humans who noticed first, of course, when their loved ones could no longer recognize them or their livers began to fail. I noticed the whales and the dolphins more than I noticed the humans—changes in behaviour, rejected calves whose mothers did not know them, their songs becoming more chaotic. The humans began to get together to discuss it and I, thinking *bloody humans are the only ones who could take something as stable and useful as a fullerene and kill the fucking planet with it,* went along. By this time they had adapted so many marine characteristics that my appearance really only provoked envy. I avoided mentioning my diet. A year or so of research and of careful sneaking about and disguising myself while reading over the shoulders of humans on trains or breaking into their houses to use technology while they snored, and we narrowed it down to my loving brother Eoghan and his money-pot, the single largest source of nanotoxins in the aquatic world.

I can smell the dawn. The black air swells with noise as soon as the first atoms of light spill over the horizon into the sea. By the time the cauterizing smell of light reaches me, I have taken refuge in the tunnels under the house, astonished that I recall them, nursing my fury at Eoghan.

Cities distress me. Urban-born—however tiny the urbs—I have always preferred cities and the relief they hold in their meeting places and talking places, their entertainments and demands for interaction, growth, dissent. But for a city to exist it must have a population and to be among the throng is hardly bearable for me now. Their heartbeats boom in my ears, with no pulse to attune to I can hear their blood gush and tumble, smell it in their skin.

When I ceased to be human, with a span of eternity before me, time slowed down. Taking up a life in the final depths of the ocean, time is barely perceptible except genetically—as we shift our atoms to make the best use of our environment—or as an evolutionary imperative—as we watch the turtles migrate, the salmon fling themselves upstream, the eels thrusting blindly to the Sargasso Sea. I have never killed a whale, though I could take a baby from the pod. I like whales. They are large and slow and I feel that they, of any mammal, exist in the same timescale as do I. They move across oceans like a human stepping across the road to a neighbour, they talk and sing and warn. Not for them the conscious display of consumption, compound conjugations, and brilliance wasted in the creation of a pretty matchbox. A swoop, a note and a thousand years of comprehension perseveres. It is simplicity sustains them. But among the humans, the air crackles with the speed of their neurons. I can hear the information surging like a forest fire through billions of synapses, chemicals thundering as they transmute, speech pouring out through the city streets, and those dreadful, terrible silences, pinpricks in the throbbing fabric, when a human ceases. I like to know that they are there, even if I am only a mote of light in the corner of their eye, but I am deafened by their presence. The tunnels beneath Forte House are cold and dark and silent but in them I hear a heartbeat.

Once in the water, my evolution began quite quickly and though I do not really understand I assume that it was because I hovered between many worlds and that concomitantly I hovered between many possibilities. I could live as Eoghan lived, feverishly trying to pretend to belong in the human world, passing as a human. I could take my revenge upon the world, terrorizing it, feeding upon it, making it sorry it had hurt my feelings. I crept out one night, rising dripping from the Corrib River, and ran off with a young girl. She was about fifteen, I guessed. I grabbed her and was instantly gone, I threw her up against a wall and ripped the shawl from her neck, in full display, while she stared at me. I could hear her poor heart fluttering, trying to beat quietly, to save its own life. I banged my head on the stone wall.

"Sorry," I said, "I thought you were something else."

I trailed back to the river, cursing myself, and slid under the water to feed instead upon fish. I found the water saved me from darkness—I could see the sun, watch it waft through green water without harming me. I began to live in the waterworld properly, not as a prison but as glorious an opportunity as America was to the rattle-boned survivors of famine and coffin-ship. I have no heartbeat, and while it is disappointing not to be able to sigh with love, an inability to breathe suddenly becomes the key to a whole world of water, where I could swim for days, as deep down as I liked, among the sorts of life forms even now the humans have never seen.

After some decades, I began to change. Years I spent crushing down the yearning for human blood. I take animal blood, a shark, a seal. They cannot see me properly, like mammals on land. Their blood is unpleasant, a taste I forced myself to acquire, and it suffices. I prepare myself to meet humans, reminding myself of our distant kinship, refusing to consider the possibility of feeling the skin pop under my teeth, feel that sudden surge of exhilarating determination, the single-pointed desire for attainment, conquest, immersion as the first salty sweet jet of blood spatters my mouth.

But if a human comes upon me without warning I cannot always control my response. I hear the pulse echo in the cold tunnel and am instantly hovering behind the source, straining to feel the unflinching artery flutter against my tongue. I dive behind a corner just in time, and am reduced to slicing my hand on a rock and pressing the slow red ooze to my lips. It is the girl from the boat.

Like gems in the palm of a hand, the water surrounds me. Like air to mortals, the water sustains me; like hope to mortals, water held me above the riptide of despair and kept me from the dark caves of death when all my life, for all eternity, seemed beyond endurance. It has been centuries since I had revenge in my heart for the brother who drank my blood and dropped me into the water. The waves near the surface are all edged with pale gold, the water is bright and clear and blue as the sky was above the clouds, before you reached the eternal darkness.

With the savaging of their world above ground, humans have begun to come to my world and the vastnesses of the expanse and depth, of the timespan that has led to these underwater mountains, this flora and fauna, humbles them. My world is as close as these humans will ever get to experiencing the unspeakable expanse of the universe. They adapt, and they step away from the world that bred them. They retain the humility that made them admit that they could no longer understand, control or participate in the world that was nominally theirs and they evolve without hesitation so that they can become part of a better one. By doing so they have made me become part of them, because they have become part of me, we are once again "us."

It is gratitude for this that drives me back to Eoghan's room. I had wanted to rescue the humans from the nanotoxins while allowing them to continue their accelerated evolution into mariners, but I realize that I will fail. He has dismissed me. As the passing of time has removed the glow from his skin, it has also removed any ability to dissemble. He has told me the absolute truth. He intends to live forever, he may cling to the physical edges of the upper world but he has adapted to the mutation of his civilization just as much as I have adapted to the physical world of the sea. He has every new technology to his wizened hand, he is engaged, at a discreet distance, in every major economic enterprise in what is left of the world. He does not care what the consequences are, because whatever they are, he will survive them. He will walk across a valley of bones, stride through the smoking landscape, but he will survive it. Even when I say *and you the only one left in the world*, Eoghan shrugs. This is a man who has staked every vampire he sired. I cannot rescue the humans, we have to rescue each other. He wants no links with either world, but I am a link, whether he likes it or not.

I dive deep to escape the afternoon sun, and I tread water there till dark. I sometimes still fantasize about dolphins and seals, basking, leaping into the sunny air, but I know of course the payment; the agony, the dust, becoming a passing skin on the surface of the ocean, like a human scattered upon a sacred river.

I am very angry with Eoghan and I recall the first time I swam in an ocean storm. I realize now, almost three hundred years later, that it was then I decided to embrace the ocean, rather than sulking on the edge of the land. The storm was in the very depths of the sea, mountainous waves and a driving, elemental force that made me think of hydrogen atoms smashing, of a blinding heat at the creation of the universe. And sex, of course; predictable, I am sorry to say, but probably unavoidable. What I had not expected was that it reminded me of when I was vampirized. I had felt cold, and light, and immobile but everything around me crashed and roared and I watched it become something other than it was. Everything I ever would have learned and everything I would have become all happened at once, my heart and brain aged, reached its peak, upon the instant. My whole being was torn apart by the gravitational pull of my new nature, and my old self and my new self spun about each other, our paths became elliptical and finally they crashed, again and again, until the new, old nature, absorbed entirely the old, young nature.

When the dark came, I broke the surface, and trod water for a while, staring first at the dead red sky, then the poisonous lights of Galway. I slipped back beneath the slick water and swam towards shore, too angry still to notice that the girl in the boat was following me.

Neither of us has noticed her entry into Eoghan's room, which considering that we are both vampires and have not fed in days, gives an idea of the rage we evoked in each other. We noticed nothing, shouting at each other, until I threw a statue at him which he deflected with a casual fury, and we both noticed the girl dance backwards to avoid the flying chunks of marble.

Eoghan and I turned, both in full display. Our throats are engorged, our breath has an aggressive, feline hiss. The inside of my mouth puffs out like an adder, and my fangs have sprung from my jawbone. Both of us are facing her, fangs stretching forward like striking snakes, our throats defensively coloured red, purple and gold, our eyes stretched and black. The vampire is dominant, close to the surface, and the human is cowering in the dark. Eoghan turns his head to follow her scent. His eyes are the eyes of a vampire. I can see her as more than a pattern of scent and heat. I see the shifting temperature patterns, but I also see her heart beat, and I see her eyes. She is staring at me, her navy eyes wide but, astonishingly, unshocked. She looks rapturous, staring at our throats. The temperature suddenly rises below her skin, her pulse booms in my ear. My throat begins to fade and my eyes to contract with the very human thought: *That girl is horny.*

But when Eoghan, glistening, lunges for her, instantly on her, I am instantly between them with a long shard of marble like a rapier in my brother's heart. There is a vacuum in the air, an indescribable noise, and nothing. Vampires do turn to dust but the difference between our time and that of a human means that their residue is already scattered like stardust into the universe by the time a human can perceive their absence. Our death is as close as we get to procreation.

The sun keeps me under the water and the weight of the water keeps her in the sun. I dress in my brother's clothes to continue the fiction of his life, then descend under Forte House, under the water, to sabotage my own efforts. She and I meet in the tremulous blue time when light and dark are mingled, on the shore, where earth and sea grind together. I keep my patience and she keeps to herself her glowing joy at witnessing evolution before her eyes, refraining, finally, from asking us to demonstrate the manifestation of the biological imperative to survive. The humans who come to Forte House can still weep for their lost loves and rail against the spinning of the world, even make a record of their thoughts and plans without ever knowing if they will be seen. I find this as alien as she finds our phosphorescence, but now they can divide up the ocean with me, agreeing without hesitation to investigate vast acreages, agreeing to meet again over expanses of time, as though it were only hours. We follow the whales and the mariners who migrate, the whale-shouldering paths wired now into our brains, collecting what we need.

I and the marine humans make the plans—who can remove the nanotoxins but leave the water capable of permitting our evolution? Who can provide us with the materials we need to repair Tor Bucky, the arches and pipes? How do we dispose of the mutant corpses—could we re-assemble the wreckages of spybots and send the corpses hurtling into space? What will happen when we stop supplying the carbon electricity to either side? I think I am the only one who wonders if it is too late and I will not say this aloud, because it is too terrifying. I can live forever, the concept of there being a *too late* is as suffoc-ating as eternal damnation.

I say nothing, because they have made me no longer just me. I know that even if the earth is ever fit to walk on again, I would not leave the ocean, even if there are already so many nanotoxins that it is too late for me and I will end my days in chaotic song, spiralling down to the sea bed. These mortals have chosen that which was forced upon me, and we are all returned to the ocean, leaving the upper world to recover as best it can. I am not bound to it, and now the mortals are bound to me because we all find a beauty in the grey cracked earth as much as we did in the purple mountains and the standing stones, because none of it can touch the immutable splendour of the vicissitudinous world that has adopted us.

Hallowtide Boar

…if the Taurids were showering the morning, they would be invisible to the shrouded city, sequinned as it was; shooting stars, burning debris, scorched the clear black sky beyond while the city mostly slept, and now the city being fuzzily awake, it was only the fog, the foggy livid sky sparkling with past rain and feebly countered by the blunted illuminations for those in motion, and of their destinations that pale and pallidly mimicked the whirling fires of the sky as the ghostly dead move in hollow mimicry of the living.

Dense fog made it difficult to tell location by looking, but B had walked the memory into her muscles over the years. Fog blurred the details. Everything hid, then loomed. Walls. Cars, rubbish-bins, those wheeled and those cemented into the footpath and dripping with damp refuse

                …vomiting crisp-
bags and cigarettes extinguished in apple-butts and
             evacuate
               voiding their cloaca
            damp refuse, and seagulls eye-
ing her bitterly, as they always did, paddling pink feet on the black rubbish-sacks slumped against the wheeled bins, and savaging the plastic to shreds

    beaks like crowbars, except yellow
             hooked
             membranous
             exposed

        shreds, the speechless in pursuit of the inedible. B stepped briskly into the road to circumnavigate the

"

birds and their prey. The green was invisible. The path revealed itself in stages, coyly revealing a curve round a building site here, a flank past a chain of blocky houses there. Without seeing much beyond a couple of anonymous metres, before she heard the rising murmur of traffic, B knew how close she was to the main road because of how long she felt she had been walking, as though she knew by bone and breath that the hour was about to strike. Here and there the street-lights were on, not so much shining as glistening. Every minor thing that was visible through this tissue of dawn seemed significant. The twilight world on display against an oyster-coloured fog

                  where is that line from? Some
kid's book. Oyster-coloured fog.
            forgetting of course that twilight
            bookends the day, twi-morning, twi-
            evening twixt.
                  …coloured fog,

      a cloud that has reached ground level.
Suspension of water droplets, that's what it was, an
obscurity in the surface layers of the atmosphere.
Saturation point of the air has been reached. The city
is beyond my event horizon.

coloured fog, the city curated. Shops coagulated on the corner, bristling with disoriented flowers thrust into buckets, with Hallowe'en masks, and bags and bales of cheap fuel. Beyond them, clouded as a scrying-ball. Just visible, the green androgyne promising safe passage

               remember one, look for a safe place,
   two don't hurry stop and wait, three…

     safe passage across the roads, though the signalling

was hostile to pedestrians, timed against maybe Usain Bolt crossing the four lanes of traffic. This grey and black morning was no morning for jay-walking

London particular, they used to say, all pipes and deerstalker hats, terraced houses behind railings, finials blunt as gravestones with glossy paint spangling with mist and creamy banks of fog overlain with velvet black shadows of rippers and the abject of respectability

jay-walking, not in this fog. Last night's midnight half-moon-light was so diffused by fog that the gauzy green had been bright as day. B was always cautious, and took the trip in two stages, waited by the stunted trees half-way. The lights turned and B clipped briskly across, and turned past the bus-stop. She always considered waiting for a bus as soon as she had to negotiate the root-ruptured footpath approaching the bus shelter, she always decided against it, and turned past to walk around by the railings. Somewhere along

yes, here, right here, abrupt and looming, blotchy and livid   whips hooping out swollen ends   amputated branches

Somewhere along here was a big elm tree, rupturing and overturning the slabs of the footpath. Fallen leaves were gathered in the tiny patch of soil, and were turning black. B. faltered. Some chance of lighting—the tree seemed backlit against the silver fog, and this clustering of birds, like tombstones along the branches, a wreath of studs in the tree-crown—grey finials, heraldry, falcons in hoods. They were parakeets, long-escaped.

The fog and the early hour muffled the world—curd-like brume in places, diaphanous veil over streetlights and shop-fronts. Blue tones and violet and the cars' sulphurous headlights creeping along. One car crept by, vibrating with drum-and-bass. Early morning traffic heavier than usual, as usual. Moonset was

> oh great parakeet to thee we cry, oh
> dum-dum-dum-dum-dum-dum-dy. That
> was some job description. Paraclete.

Moonset was passed, sunrise in an hour, sun rising into a gritty dimness, and likely lurking there all day, oozing its veiled light from just over the horizon, then, raging orange like an infected eye, it would sink. B clipped along, her shoes ringing tightly like a distant and anonymous engine. She turned right auto-matically, turned left, scuttled across road. All the bus shelters were full, and she turned right, with the faintest sense of smugness, because the short-cut through the Gardens was faster than any bus. A chipper, an under-taker, some random

> masks pressed to the shop windows, plastic
> corrugations and carmine streamers for hair. Hallowe'en.
> Christmas decorations in boxes at the back, straining at
> the leash for Hallowe'en to give way, stretching and
> limbering for the indecorous bolt to the shelves and
> across the walls, lodging themselves in the window-
> frames, twinkling winningly in the blurred street-lights.

> some random

local shops. A sudden noise like ripping cloth made her look back. The parakeets had

> miles back. *Miles.*

> had been startled and had flown up and

out of the tree. The light was too dim to reflect anything except fragments of green from their feathers, green was smudged with the shadows. Emeralds handled by sooty fingers. Scattered like light fragments flung into the murk.

The traffic lights shut down the amber and ignited the red. They blazed dully through the gloom. B marched across the pedestrian crossing, and turned at last to the gates of the Botanic Gardens. All of the gates were locked. There was a very narrow stile, though, previously barred but now open to those who knew the discreet means of unlocking the loose bolt. Strictly speaking, of course, this was illegal. An embossed iron plaque adorned each gate, announcing that the Gardens would open at sunrise each day and close again at sunset

> embossed on iron dewy damp-spangled
> iron, times that are moveable feasts, different
> seconds each day

again at sunset. But it wasn't really illegal, not illegal-illegal. B was only one of many of the besuited that only became law-abiding again once they had reached the north gate, by which time the sun had hitched itself up over the horizon and the gates had been opened. It was a short walk from the stile to the north gate, and the office was only three minutes further. It was convenient. It would be sunrise by then.

The ground between the railing and the sweep of sign-posted path was rough and gravelly. B lifted her heels out of the rubble and toddled. The trees closest to here were bright-barked birches turning out the silver side of their last leaves. They loomed, they and the cracked beeches, and then sank back. The path was immaculately maintained, branching often, and on clear days the familiar passing eye saw the flags of almost every part of the Gardens: the canopy of yew that sheltered the fragile Japanese Garden, the wrought iron ridge of the Glass House, or the rounded crowns of the beech trees outside the Walled Garden, and so forth. Today there was nothing but fog, a steel lake of it blending with the iron sky, a dome pulled

                    petrichor, is that it? When
        the air tastes metallic   or was that the
        food of the gods? Ichor. Ichor-iko -i -
        nay. Koh-i-Noor. Tastes of iron, anyway.

    pulled over the city, and everything was muffled, even
the sounds of cars, the creaking and hissing of buses. The hard
surface glistened, with fog, or dew, and curved

    is this right? Thought it was all in a straight line. Curve?

                        curved to left and right,
and trees loomed pallidly and retreated.

    Somewhere, and a long way away, a woodpecker was batter-
ing the bole of a tree. There was no wind to speak of, so B
supposed that the rustling was night animals on their rounds.
There was more rustling, but not so much that it challenged
B's brisk steps. It was still too dark and the mist too thick to
see anything. The path ran through an alley of yew trees, instantly quieter and darker, the ground soft with fallen needles.
The cold and the fog had burned everything from the air,
except that faint metallic trace. B walked in virtual silence

        mother of Christ—God forgive me—rats aren't that
        size no cats aren't silver though.
                    Rats: silver; magpie: black and white and
                quick iridescence;
        except that must surely be a dog, that harsh panting

                        silence. The
gardens had the same palette as the street but it had practically
no lights to fox the fog with aureoles. Somewhere, again,
somewhere else, a woodpecker battered the tree and somewhere closer, much, much closer, a magpie rattled, cackled. B
realized that

too dim to see any iridescence   pity   just black
and that unblemished white flash

B

realized that she recognized the part of the Gardens that she
was now approaching, and she felt a tingle of shock, and in
the moment of suspension after a shock, in which all perspective and recognition is lost and must be re-discovered, she felt
a rush of delight. The crowns of the trees that surrounded the
Quincunx Meadow were lost in the bluish mist. The path was
narrower here than she recalled, so the trunks of the beech
trees clustered on either side and their branches locked over
her head. B stopped, and looked up, hanging her head right
back. But the mist was too dense to see any stars. The
undersides of the leaves looked silver, and oddly bright, given
there was no light. Something rustled overhead, fluttering,
and—reminded of birds and the blessings they bestrew on
passers-by beneath—B hastily closed her mouth and lowered
her head. The path sloped steeply

                        disconcertingly close,
    straight across—gauzy cloud, gauze crumpled, no,
    whirled, stirred, gauze and a breeze, trees and some
    buildings all filmy in dim light
            the sky is beyond the day's event horizon,
    replaced by a matt dome closed over us

                    and then suddenly and whoosh those
    are *fireworks* and down they tinkle, sparkling, embellishing
    the smoky morning with sequins
        grace notes descending   clinquant streamers the
    silver sides of the leaves on the black trunks the gold
    spatterings of fire down the grey gown of morning

            path sloped steeply down into a puddle of fog,

drew the eye across, tricked it briefly, a *trompe-l'œil* continuation. In reality, the path sloped down and in the hollow before it began to rise again, there was an ancient yew tree. A tree with personality, B saw as she approached, a remarkable tree. It was yew, not a tall tree but a wide one, a trunk of almost twenty feet round and looking more like it was made of many pillars built on top of each other, or of tall, smooth round animals huddling together, than a tree that grew all of a piece. It was only about ten or twelve feet tall, a baby compared to the pines and beech and the vast elm, but its spread was wide. Its branches sprawled over the space of a small house, keeping the sun off the ground and strewing the earth with dark green needles. Disconcerted, B stopped again. She stepped

loved the yew trees, and those sinuous forms

complicated knotted animals in medieval pictures, dense shadows. How can you forget this? So thoroughly. Forgetting the year you were born in, as though never knowing it. A betrayal

She stepped off the path to pay proper homage. The glowing red berries were subdued and ashy in the veiled morning, but she pictured them easily like gleaming cups, brimming poison though they were. One fell into her palm, and she put it into her pocket

taxine, that was it. Or was that the name of a Dolly Parton song? *Your beauty is beyond compare…dah-dah-dah-dah…compete with you, Taxine.*

Now B remembered why she remembered the path. She had come through here before with an elderly aunt, now deceased, who had wanted to see the outdoor art installed by the Public Monuments Department. Aunt Min had mortified her by crawling into a little snail-shaped house made of willow-wands and issuing an order to B to keep sketch.

"I'm ninety-six," Min had retorted, when B tried to hurry her along by invoking the spectre of approaching authority, "what are they going to do to me?"

The snail-shaped house of willow was still there, and the honeycomb made of something or other symbolic was still hanging from a tree. It looked very stark now, the fog and the early morning draining away its colour and leaving it like ashes and velvet. Whatever it was made of was dry and papery, and made a soft, ambiguous rustling noise. The house of willow was so fractured by fog and shadow that it looked made of textile or wool, but the faint grinding, and squeaking was either its wooden whips rubbing together, or over-excited mice. Behind it were the tall grasses of the Quincunx Meadow. B hesitated

> *Good of you to take one for the team* is what
> he'd said   *make yourself indispensable* advice Mam
> specialized in   but a bit difficult to put into practice
> with everything nailed in the performance review
>   recollection of office-life from her
> joyous days in the advertising agency in Oxford in
>   when?
>   *That was long ago, back in nineteen-fifty-and-*
> *frozen-to-death.* He wasn't looking for indispensable,
>   Rob, *he* was indispensable   dreading the day a transfer

hesitated and decided there was not conceivably time to visit the artworks again. Another time.

In almost the same moment, B heard the ring-tone of a phone

not a phone ringing, a ring-tone,
everything signals to something else,
intangibility is progress, immateriality is

a

phone, and turned to see that Giggler was approaching the Yew Way from the west. B was smacked to a halt, like she had walked into a door. The walk through the Gardens was always a solitary walk. On one occasion only had she had company, and that was Giggler, running to catch up with B, reminding her of their meeting briefly at the pub 'the other night' when someone was getting married, having a birthday, or a baby, or something. Pulling the buds from her ears as she jogged to a halt Giggler had commented on the opening and closing times, their chunky life in the iron plaque, their shifting specificity.

"It's like the stars you see being dead stars," she had said, smiling, and B had smiled back, bewildered.

The stars we see are four thousand years old.
If the sun exploded, we would see it for eight minutes
after it was gone. Speed of light. Is that true?

"Light takes eight minutes to travel from the sun to us," Giggler had explained, her smile fading like a morning star, "It takes about eight minutes to walk from here to the other gate. So, by the time we arrive, we will be obeying the rules. We're just pre-empting our future selves."

The walk after that had been eight minutes of excruciating silence.

Without thinking now, B turned away from the Yew Way, away from the sound of the phone, and the hoarse approaching voice, onto the wood-mulch path, towards the Quincunx Meadow. The creaking rattle of a magpie trailed her.

The tall grasses soughed terribly softly.

softly terribly

The sturdy grasses circling the clearing were tall, and hollow as well as thick like stalks of straw. The fog was still impenetrable, but a light lightening of the violet-black sky to a dense ultramarine was just visible—or if not visible, sensible—over the art exhibition's central feature: a meadow had been mown into a quincunx. Simultaneously, the sky elsewhere darkened. It became grainy, flakes of dark drifting closer and closer together, in viscous, glassy light. Grasses ceased to seem domestic when higher than head-height and stretching farther than the reach of sight.

Hallowe'en in the gloaming.
Domestic, yes, familiar, but not at the point
of the day when light and dark were bleeding into one
like watercolours on a page, and at a time in the year
when that which was, and that which might be, that
which is, blending and parting like scents on a path
superstition

Dark things darted in the pale grasses, angular shadows, the smell of wild things, rushing heat, stiff fur scratching, heavy small things scampering, the woolly fragments of damp mulch ground under feet, then the grasses on the other side snapping. B followed the turn in the path, again, again. Fragments of earth or peat scattered over her boots, something panted, scraped. Crouching, she peered into the grass. Some cream and black shape stopped, eye glittering. It contorted itself, flickered from sight.

There was no change in or lightening of the sky. The woodchip mulch on the path was dark as plums. The low rosettes of grass that lined it shining orange, burning red. Behind them, the long border grasses were green as apples, streaked with bright whites and sandy yellows, streaked with umber, and violet. The grasses twitched and swayed abruptly, and thin sprays of earth bloomed onto the path. B glimpsed only shadows again, again the gamey smell of wildness. Strangely shaped, low to the ground, and long, limbs out at angles, scuttling, pulsing leaping-frog's progress. B looked, but it had vanished. A sound boomed, distending the taut silence. Another flash, a smear of crimson, and shimmering streaking black, looming, leaping long-legged across the high streaked grass, into the shaved quincunx of the meadow. B followed.

The boar, when she found it, was stunning. The wood showed every hatchet-stroke and burn-mark. The wooden fore-quarters were monumental, and the hindquarters almost delicate. A spiky blackthorn mane, jutting aggressively out at the front, and narrowed to a ridge that trailed away down the bulky spine. Its face was mask-like. The perfunctory slashes that made its almond-shaped eyes tilted them up at a fantastical angle. Its ears were big, tufted things, round like radars, and with holes roughly bored. It looked barely uncovered, a boar bursting out from an oak chrysalis, kicking its tangled exoskeleton away behind it. The only thing with fine detail was its snout.

The boar was made of oak, shining in the odd light, even the parts of it—the face and the hindquarters—that had some bog-oak embedded in them were gleaming. The eyes were mosaics of tiny slivers of red or black or white stone, and the ridge of blackthorn-hair was black, gleaming with moisture, and here and there flares of red and yellow, where leaves had pocketed the last of the sun. The black mouth was roughly cut. The whole animal shone like honey in sunlight, stiff and still as it was, the blocky and jagged muscles, only vaguely resembling those of a live body, quivering with power. The grass on which it stood was dying with the year, but with a last vigorous display, matching the sunny gold of the turning blackberry leaves undimmed by the fog. There were saplings nearby, smooth and round, and so bright a brown

> crepuscular rays, is what they would be called, if
> light rather than trees, aureole

so bright a brown that they almost shone. B pulled herself together. It was still a statue, or carving, work of art anyway, a work. It was the setting, or the combination of the two, that was disconcerting. She cast about her for any signs that approaching the works of art was prohibited

Aunt Min, God bless her

prohibited, and finding that there were none, she stepped from the mulch-covered path, and crossed the shaved circle towards the boar. Her feet ground and crunched on the bristly grass. Fog spangled the glittering eye.

The snout was a work of perfection. It shone, the wood having been polished and the hairs represented by filaments of gold tucked together. The nostrils were lined with slivers of red glass, and with threads and twists of silver and gold. B leaned over to look more closely, but

pig snouts more sensitive than dogs'.
Twenty feet underground, they can smell some-thing at twenty feet   I think he said   miles? what's twenty-five miles down?

but stumbled. Or slipped, maybe. Tripped. Or been tripped, that same rush of heat, the gamey smell. Either way, whatever it was, she was flat on her back on the stubble, the last gasp of air knocked out of her and

playing, a platform they were using for painting the apex of the gable wall,
don't be climbing on that, but that was irrelevant, a rule as random as a torn cloud, and not meant for
before you know it, the ground rushes up, and flat on her back on the gravel, thinking *if I'm killed, she'll kill me, in so much trouble*

the last gasp of air knocked out of her, and her head ringing like a rubbed glass where she had struck it against the ground, but she was otherwise unhurt. B sat up. No; her shoulder hurt badly, and the ball ground in the socket when she gyrated it gently. It was her left shoulder. She had fallen on her right side. She flexed her fingers, and rotated her wrist, and nothing seemed damaged, but her shoulder was tender and painful. She started

hit it when I fell?

Such a peculiar

thing, to fall. Falling.

The characteristic of youth, and of

age. The rest of the time

ball-bearings run along their chutes.

She started to get up, leaning on her steady palm, dragging grooves in the ground with her heels. She was showered down the back with crumbs and splinters and flying chips of mulch and was almost overturned. She rolled, and squatted. A blackness flashed out, black and crimson, violent and over-powering, like a lightning strike. It leaped the boar, vanished, a momentary smear of burning red on the pearlescent grey sky, and then as though it had never been. B's heart pounded on. Her

afterglow, migraine

intense, intense,

Matisse

Her eyes rang, too, in their way, they ached, and when she closed them up tight to relieve them, all the colours pulsed, and all the shapes were senseless. The

compelling, mesmerising, that

was it, mesmeric.

The boar had turned. The world was fracturing in its wake, splitting and assembling itself, splitting and assembling

How do you leave its presence?

The boar was gone, or mostly gone, gone from its place at least, the space was unfilled but the time was crowded, the seconds jammed with its absence and her failure to comprehend—

Fear will drive you out, that's how. Fear and disbelief.

The boar returned. The boar was exactly as she remembered it, elegant-hoofed, wooden, monumental.

B's access-card beeped in the reader. She noted the time on the screen. The lift hummed as it descended. The arrow over the door lit up. The door beeped. It opened. B stepped in, and pressed the button for the fourth floor. The doors were silent, and the lift hummed on the ascent.

The lights in the open-plan office were motion-sensitive, and flickered as she walked through. Overhead, the air-conditioning was whirring. Printers and photocopiers were arrayed in an alcove to her left. They whirred, too, and clicked anonymously. Faintly, there came a beep, suggestive of malfunction.

B's own desk was spotless. She dipped her fingerprint into the pot-plant's compost, and decided it did not need to be watered. Every compartment of her desk-tidy was complete. On her right, she had a photograph in a frame, and she had tucked her mug behind it. Switching on her computer with one hand, she picked up the mug with the other, and started off for the canteen. Lights flicked on as she walked, the machines whirred and clicked and beeped, and overhead, the air-conditioning whirred, too. The lift hummed as it descended. The arrow over the door it up. The door beeped. It opened. B stepped in, and pressed the button for the ground floor. The doors were silent, and the lift hummed on the descent.

Hummed. Descended. Lit up. Beeped. Opened. Stepped. Pressed. Silent. Hummed. Ascended. Flickered. Whirred. Arrayed. Whirred, too. Clicked. Beeped. Suggestive.

Even before the lights flickered on, B could see that something had been added to her desk. There was a sheaf of papers, of a denseness that told her immediately it was something she was being asked to review, a policy, or, more likely, a work instruction, an operating procedure. Her diary and task-list, side-by-side on the computer screen, were already open. She typed in the name of the procedure, and the date on which it had to be returned.

<blockquote>sickening for something? Time of the year for it.</blockquote>

The light outside was still crepuscular, a grainy, gauzy dark lavender. Very distantly, there were flashes of fireworks, their burning streamers, their intense, brief flares like stars through the fog. Even the windows opposite were blurred, the lights in them, like looking at them through tears. The green of the pot-plant was opaque, too, the hooping blades of sharp-edged grass were dusty. B turned her attention to her list, clicking

<blockquote>always a comfort, a list. Lists of everything—threw them all away of course—lists of moth species, of capital cities, mountain ranges, fungi, spices, soil protozoa, precious stones, herbs. A childish thing, to need so intangible a control over the crashing chaos of the day</blockquote>

<blockquote>clicking</blockquote>

the corner of the screen so that the task-list sank down obediently out of sight. The departmental head needed the rota done early, last week's team meeting minutes to be sent out, and a diplomatic email sent, to undo the head of steam building up because of the section head's inability to refrain from spitting out his soother. There was the list. There were the draft minutes. The rota. As each task was completed, the software would register it as being complete, and the colours on her task list changed, bringing everything in the day under control

> actually
> there isn't really order, or control, it's
> King Cnut trying to *lever a few more minutes into*
> *the day* and the incoming waves and the rising
> tide and stuffing progress reports and project
> plans and operating procedures into the split in
> the dam

everything in the day under control. B struck two keys on her keyboard in quick succession, and the rota came up on her screen. It was colour-coded, too. B looked at it, trying

> trying to remember this
> > bizarre image, a hundred years ago, a toy,
> > red and green plastic squares, to be pushed into
> > a pattern

trying to remember which colours stood for which member of staff. She pressed her fingerprint into the base of the potted grass again. It was too dry. The green was fogged with dust, and the edges as sharp as blades. They scratched gently at her hand. B opened her bag and took out a cotton handkerchief, and began wiping away the dust. Twice she stopped, and looked into the dry ceramic tub in which the plant sat, taking it out, even, to see if there were woodlice or some other infesting insect scratching about, rustling. When she had finished cleaning the leaves, she took the tub to the water-cooler to fill it. As it filled, she wondered if the water was too cold. She brought the tub into the lavatory, and mixed in some

> be testing it on your wrist yet,
> like Biddens told you to the one time
> you baby-sat Nell. What are you
> doing

> mixed

in some hot water. She walked very briskly back to her desk, alert to the fact that time had been lost. The briskness was not just about speed, returning quickly to what needed to be done, but about attitude, and focus.

B returned the tub to its corner, and tucked a tissue underneath it, then returned the glossy-leaved plant to the tub. It scratched at her fingers. Her reflection beside her in the window was very sharp, but fragmented where her dark suit blended with the darkness of the world. The window reflected like a photograph, in layers. Behind her own hands, face, and all the rest of it, B could see the lights of the city, smudged by the fog. The sky, grainy and burnt-looking, the sun unrisen. The windows of the offices and shops, the cars creeping along, like ships forging ahead despite everything. Without warning, a bird was suddenly splayed against the window, bright eye, speckled, multi-coloured feathers, blue and gold, black. B released a chirrup of alarm. The bird huddled. As abruptly as it had struck the glass, it flew away. B was relieved that

> don't break their necks they can still fly, but
> brain injury   fall from the sky
> fall of a sparrow fall to the ground dead

> was relieved

that the bird seemed to be unharmed. She straightened every-thing else—desk-tidy, in-out trays, monitor, key-board, print-outs—and started working out the rota.

Lights flickered on. The dark and concentrated world fractured, then instantly reassembled: a bright, active place, demanding attention and response. Someone was striding towards the desks, carrying rustling bags and trailing scintillat-ing helium balloons. B was briefly unable to recall the woman's name, and nerves jangled in her hands at the absolute absence of any hint of what it might be, as though she came unexpect-edly upon the edge of a chasm.

"Hiya!" said the newcomer, and deviated for an instant from her path, as though to approach B's desk, but then returned to her course, saying, "I'll chat'cha in a minute, set these down first."

Even looking at the rota did not answer the question of identity. Brands and influencers had coated so many of the staff with unlikely skin tones and veneered teeth that they all looked the same. While B equated that with the rock-hard crests, chained silver-plate, and velvet swathes of her own youth, she now understood the embarrassed bewilderment with which her father had gazed about him when picking her up after social events—he had no idea which quasi-Victorian banshee was his own.

thank the baby jesus—Cora. Her
name is Cora

Soft thumps, as of snow drifting, came from Cora's desk, and

Cora, Corisande of the circus, Koré

and
an unceasing, gurgling stream of muttering accompanied it, Cora seemed to be sifting through her purchases

god my feet hurt. Really, really hurt. Why on
earth these shoes are   foot growing into a point.

sifting through her purchases. B returned
to her

to see if she had everything they had agreed on
stuck with this shit again, just
right to say I should say no but she
doesn't understand how   fucking string-poppers
can't believe I forgot   of fucking Sheba and her
song and dance

returned
to her rota, sketching out possible combinations on a sheet of
paper. She had no

can't stop now though, it's the suit you're
in, however badly it fits. Badly-Fitting B-Suit. Ha! The
whole wearisome fandangle though, the

She had no recollection of whose birthday it was today,
though she could recall signing the card, yet another card, but
had somehow thought it was to mark the arrival of a baby. Or
possibly a wedding. But it was not, it was a birthday. There
would be streamers, and metallic-coated confetti, and tiny
sweets, each twisted in plastic, all over the desk and the keyboard. Cora strode down to B's desk and hooked her hands
on the corner of the partition, so as to lean in.

"I'm after setting up the birthday stuff on Bunty's desk,"
she said, "And I'm having second thoughts about the balloons.
Will you come and look?"

Bewildered, and uneasy, B followed her to the decorated
desk.

"They have the age on them," Cora said, "D'ye see? D'you

think she'll mind? She won't, will she? What do you think? Would you mind?"
Christ, she'll think I'm
saying she's old Christ
B stared at her, unable to answer. She would have

Mind? Mind? Bunty? Who minds? Thirty? Thirty's nothing. Forty was nothing. Fifty will be nothing when it comes to it. Why would I know what this Bunty person thinks? What do I say? What do I say? This shit is hideous. Say something. Bin the lot, and say no more about it.

She would have minded extravagantly if someone had dumped all this crap on her desk. But where the birthday girl worked was habitually cluttered with books, and gloves, and flyers for musicals, advertisements for skin-care, train itineraries, bus timetables, packets of tissues, crumpled papers, scrawled reminders to herself to phone, email or ask someone, tiny tinted bottles of herbal remedies, boxes of painkillers, tubes of vitamins, inspirational quotations, sun-glasses, and, bizarrely, an antique fob-watch of Mullingar pewter, that to have an extra archaeological layer of the waste products of celebration hardly seemed to matter.

"Uh—well—"

"Would you do it?" Cora asked, with the air of getting down to simple brass tacks, "Would you put up those balloons?"

"Mmm. No."

cold it smells, the frost has extracted something
from the air. Something metallic. Iron. Mercury.

Cora wrinkled up her fake-tanned nose, and contemplated the balloons with her head on one side. There were three of them, each one gold, with 'You Are 30!' on them in crimson, navy, and emerald green.

God almighty the shit you have
to give a fuck about in this place   doctor
mirabilis   forever at hares and hounds after
matters men are forbidden to know   balloons
christ

Cora said,

"Nah…you know, I think I'll leave them. Wouldn't that be okay? It's just a bit of fun. If she doesn't like them, I can always take them down later. That'd do, wouldn't it?"

"Mmm. Yes."

"I'm going to get a coffee, can

                                                    What is the matter? Cat got
                    your tongue?
                        grandmother's phrase   convinced it was literal
         meaning   Gram's cracked voice wobbly stern not
         unkindly   image of a black-and-white cat pouncing
         on, batting, wrestling with still lively, flapping tongue

"I'm going to get a coffee, can I get you anything?"

They went together. Every time a door opened or closed, lights snapped on or flickered out. Cora clumped carefully down the stairs behind B, berating herself for wearing stacked heels. In the canteen, Cora was instantly subsumed into a small group of new staff, perching sideways on the edge of her chair as a sign of imminent departure, while B made herself some tea from her own stash of teabags, and waved to Cora

                    wearied by the whole fandangle of loyalty to
            these doubtful gods but if not them, then who? To
            abandon the shrine was to invite formlessness and
            chaos

                        and waved to Cora as she
went out, remembering, as she went upstairs, that—given her

grade—she should have hovered meaningfully, an embodied reminder to Cora to cease her chatter and get back to her desk.
Rota, rotisserie, rotunda, Rottweiler, file, fillet, *file*,
Is mise Raifteirí an file, lán dóchais is grá
there were days, because I have heard tell of them, that these things mattered
Cora, Josh, Mercy, Emmie, Ish
Fuck, Thursday. Emmie off, sodding stats report Thursday. Fuckedy-fuck-fuck-fuck
Ag seinm ceol do phocaí folamh. Unmediated, that was it. Unmediated. What's this, against a blind man's poetry for a destitute audience? We are underfunded, understaffed, underappreciated. Stats, reports, rotas—soothers and comfort blankets for senior—

B put down her pen, and immediately picked it up again. She straightened her keyboard, and pulled the requisition forms closer. The moment

If not the whole grisly quadrille of alarm clocks and hurried breakfasts,
ill-fitting B suits
thin-soled shoes, dusting on
Saturday, ironing on Sunday, counting on Friday, then what?

The moment she had sent round the rota, after the files were ordered, and just as she started the cross-training schedule for new staff, Rob strode in in his cycling gear, his ear-buds leaking raucous sound. Lights flashed on, and flashed off the reflective bands on his clothes and around his ankles. He always started ripping asunder his fastenings as he was walking into his office.
Maybe he'll emerge as Superman.

B snorted, and hastily texted *Rob's arrived* to Cora, and started on the diplomatic email. Rob pulled down the blind in his office so he could change, and Cora was back at her desk before he and his chivvying bonhomie emerged. The layers of the window's reflections were blended now. Here and there, down the river and above the copper parabola of a distant church, the fireworks bloomed briefly and trailed, fading, away. The fog and the dawn twilight began to withdraw their amethyst hides from the window-panes.

                                             flakes of fireworks
        falling like stars   not stars really burning dust and
        debris   meteors   right time of year for the
Taurids? Too early too late?
            maybe they are cascading down behind the
      fog the mist blazing away unseen   by
                 Taurids

It was a busy day. Rob emerged from his office long enough to tell B that Lauren Someone's supervisor had rung in sick, and that B should take Lauren for the day.

"Let her shadow you," he said, "Learning by doing's the name of the game. Higher-Ups very keen on speedy onboard-ing."

                         …bloody word is on-
      boarding? On-boarding. Skate-boarding. Water-
      boarding
          Too early for Taurids. Orionids
      are before them.
                    Comet. Year?

"I expect her to be able to take over setting up the remote meetings by tomorrow. This afternoon, no reason why not."

Because she has to learn seven procedures all rendered unnecessarily convoluted because the equipment is cheap and shows it, the technology is—

"Uh-mmm. Sure."

Rob disappeared. Two people in the pod behind B came back from tea-break, walking slowly and talking loudly of the easing of traffic during holidays, talking of talk of vaccines and travel shots and an emergency treatment. B escaped by bringing her mug back to the canteen, and on the way, she stopped in the lavatory, where three colleagues were strung across the passage diarizing something, so to cover her retreat, B took some hand-cream. Having regained

> What will there be to say of me when I'm
> dead? Keep your hands soft and feminine, even
> when walking with the shades
> > Then the Leonids. Last of
> > the year
> > > No, the Ursids.

Having regained their desks, the two chatterers were joined by a male colleague, recently a father, and conversation turned to cracked nipples and breast-pumps. B stuck her finger in her ear, taking a succession of service requests into the other. She pinned the receiver to her free ear with her shoulder, filling in the form with her free hand. The photocopier behind her was on the blink again. It was so advanced that no-one could so much as change the toner, and now it was uttering aggressive, plaintive bleats for attention. B looked at the clock on her computer. She was

> —What will they put on my gravestone?

> She was late for tea break,

and so could sit on her own. She read a book that some-one

had left behind them, on preserving fruit and vegetables. The Head of Unit came in, and sat down while saying *okay if I sit here?* Roy was conscientious about the CEO's injunction to 'break up the silos' and 'flatten the hierarchy.'

"Preserving, very enterprising," he said, rapidly buttering a sloping scone the size of his hand, "Bet you're a dab hand with the home-mades. Eh?"

He reached out a buttery finger, and wiped it across the cover of the book several times, trying to draw it to himself. Finally, B shoved it almost onto his plate.

"You know, don't you, that there is no economic value in preserving your own food?" he said, "You know that, don't you? No, really, it's true. Think about it."

Before she had a moment to think of an excuse to get away, he had

> Quadrantids, Lyrids, Eta Aquariids,
> Delta Aquariids
>> Alpha Capricornids
>> Perseids
>> Draconids
>> Orionids, Taurids, Leonids
>> Ursids
>> Geminids, Ursids

get away, he had launched into a lecture. B finished her tea rapidly. There was no pause until he had ended with,

"You shouldn't read those kinds of books. They're just money-makers for some, you know, influencer."

He held up his fingers, drooping like the ears of a dis-appointed dog.

"The library's only around the corner," he said, "Get some good travel books. You'd enjoy them. What's his name? Michael Palin. That other chap and his wife, God love her. Great Canal Journeys."

I'd enjoy them. *I'd enjoy them.* This is chaos. This is random. Burning debris falling from the sky

"Sorry," said B, "Rob's looking for me."
"Oh—oh fine, fine," Roy said, relieved.
B trotted upstairs behind Rob, hardly able to hear him over the clattering of their heels. She nodded along, making mental notes, making bright little affirmative noises.

The day rattled on. The fog peeled away from the city, but haunted it, lurking in sheltered places and seasoning the air with iron. The footpaths were indefinably greasy, and slippy when B walked to the top of the street at lunchtime to buy a sandwich. It was a rotten little place she went to, harshly-lit and garish. The counter where the food was prepared was boiling hot, and at lunchtimes, there was always a queue of teenagers in school uniforms. B cursed herself for not remembering to get a sandwich in the morning, and joined the queue. It always moved slowly. Most people made up their minds only when it was their turn to select, and the sight of choice available seemed to rob them of

should be above my pay-grade to come in to work that early but he is so certain it is below his to do this kind of work   what can you say to his *good of you to take one for the team* and his *value your support*, and all the rest of that fugitive finery that fails to deliver a cent more or a minute extra   a form of conspiracy
pretending business is all about real things and the way things are   all rhetoric, all manipulation
gas-lighting   the world is gaslit

rob them of all capacity to make a decision. Ships approached icebergs, nuclear warning systems malfunctioned, while each customer havered over sun-dried tomatoes and bloated, brutalized chicken. While she waited, B became conscious of something in her shoe. It was a piece of wood-mulch. She removed it, and looked

> the whole world, gas-lit, all these children,
> all these people who were once children, all told
> they could be happy, be themselves, be fulfilled
> and all they will ever be is working for someone
> else

> and looked around for a bin. There was one in the corner by the door, she would have to hold the fragment in her hand until she was leaving. B inched up the queue. Someone shrieked with laughter behind her. Someone up ahead of her blushed and shuffled when his voice

> incessant insistence on coupledom and
> babies—solitary celibates aren't a good business plan
> for consumer

and shuffled when his voice suddenly boomed when he was asking for mayonnaise. The queue shuffled up. B glanced at her watch, and made a face, unobserved by an indifferent world. She regulated her time-keeping very tightly, keeping a close eye on the flexi-time so she could build up the extra day

> wage-slaves. No autonomy, everything bound by
> or wage-indentured-servant, at least.

build up the extra day, but today she would have to take a longer lunch. The queue unravelled briefly when a group travelling together broke apart in mock fighting. B stepped back patiently, and glanced

> archetype   wrangle the hair, painted the face,
> even a separate wardrobe in the spare room   plastic
> covers

> shoehorns and everything.

Office Worker, down to the last apotropaic button

patiently,
and glanced down at the obstruction under her foot. It was
another piece of mulch, a thick fragment. There were several
pieces, a little heap, scattered

dusting on Saturdays, ironing on Sunday,
counting on Friday
week nearly over, life with it, a break from
these bizarre shoes, and the badly cut, badly designed
second skin

second skin.

a little heap, scattered around her feet. People behind
her kicked some of the fragments away. The queue moved
forward. Murmuring began. It was B's turn to order. She always
knew

the hell is it all coming from?

always
knew what she was going to order. A white bread sandwich,
with tuna mayonnaise, tomatoes

salt and flour so low-grade it could be
swept   up from the floor

tuna mayonnaise, tomatoes, and cheese

how can any real thing be this cheap?
Tuna leaping in Mediterranean waters

and cheese. The slices of bread
were enormous. The mounds of pale tuna mayonnaise were
huge, too, expertly squashed down by the solemn-faced server.
It was usually the same person, very solemn-faced, very quick.
A mound of

is the wind blowing this stuff in?

mound of pale cheese

awful programme about feed-stalls and cows being
slaughtered for not churning out a calf a year

mound of pale cheese, and circles of flabby tomato arranged
on top. The murmuring was growing louder. B looked down
again. There was mulch dust on the backs of her legs, and a
little pile of it, dark amber and soft, around her shoes. She looked
down along the queue, older people kicking the stuff irritably
to one side, the teenagers acting out amazement, gazing open-
mouthed at each other.

probably not here though, you always
see cattle out in the fields   green fields dairy
probably imported anyway   big Dutch
cows, Friesans   happy as pigs in shit

"They don't like shit, actually," said the server, busy cutting
the enormous sandwich into triangles.
"Heh?"
"Pigs," she said, deftly wrapping it up in greaseproof paper,
"They're very clean. They have latrines. People think they are
dirty, but they're not. They use mud to protect their skin."
She weighed the sandwich. B shook her foot free of mulch.
The server came back, sticking a label to the paper, and
handed over the parcel of food.
"They've no sweat glands, you see," she said. B said impuls-
ively, shaking the other foot,
"Like the Duke of York?"
The woman smiled, wrinkling up her nose.
"Rather be stuck in a lift with a pig," she said. She nodded
at the lake, the stream, of mulch on the floor.

"Don't worry about it," she said, "Happens more than you think."

She smiled again. Her earrings dazzled. Then she was solemn again, nodding to the next customer to give their order. B strode over to the cash-counter, slipping and tottering on the uneven, mulched floor, but determinedly pretending it was the usual tiled surface. She paid for the food, and went out. All the way back to the office, she had as an earworm a jingle she had read on Twitter:

Oh, the grand old Duke of York
He borrowed twelve million quid,
He gave it to someone he never met,
For something he never did.

That afternoon, they had a presentation for Bunty's birthday. She had been delighted with the state of her desk, and with the balloons, the present. There was cake, and finger-food, and Cora kept the conversational balls in the air so that everyone made appropriate noises, filtered through cake, to being told holiday plans and birthday gifts.

"We're going to pop round to O'Callaghan's later," Cora said, "If anyone wants to join us."

There was murmured agreement, and Cora launched into an account of the pub's refurbishment at the start of the summer. Long-serving staff recounted memories of previous favourite pubs, the pubs eventually vying for position as best pub, the champion for The Gravedigger seeing off competition from Mulligan's—full of pretentious yuppies pretending to be Dubs; Davy Byrne's—full of pretentious arts students thinking they were Joyce, and dazed Americans thinking they were in Galway; Doheny & Nesbitts—full of bloody civil servants—

> hated literally every pub I've ever been in that
> awful place everyone loved in Galway   everyone
> said it was *great craic* meaning noisy and awful

Nesbitts—full of bloody civil
servants, but had to admit a soft spot for the toasties with
mustard in Grogans

only pub ever was that place out in the middle of
nowhere , Dowling's, Doolin's, as they pronounced it,
quiet, quiet   huge fire, the publican played the fiddle
later   like a scene from something

B slipped away, and returned to her desk.

Darkness and the fog returned. Cora was the particle around
which all of the others began to cohere, winding on their
scarves, pulling on their coats. She kept looking at her watch,
and when one of the clerks went
Like trying to manage frog's spawn

one of the clerks went to see where the two editors had
got to, Cora went to B's desk by the window, and was startled
to see the post deserted. She was not a snooper, but thought
that the sheet of paper left over the keyboard was a note to
someone, so she picked it up.

What will my tombstone say of me? Well,
there's…there's...
'The skin was as smooth as ~~sil~~   ~~pea~~   hyacinths.
Hyacinths, wild wild'
'Always glow and be ageless, as you move among the
shades of the dead.'

Perfect ball-bearings strain obediently
in flawed cogs   a perfect life a perfect drought
of even imperfect meaning

Cor turned the page over, more as a gesture of disbelief than
in expectation of there being more words.

'A chorus for this time: give me honey with no bee, plunder the hive till fruitless apple-blossoms spin down to the black earth, the birds fall and the stars are quenched.'

Co was shaken, and bemused. She put

don't cover this in first aid. What sort of emergency responder does this need? What would go on the back of the hi-vis vest?

She put down the paper, and looked around. No-one else had noticed her presence or B's absence. At the far side of the room, the fire-door was open the slightest crack.

…garlanded? What   crown when the sea boils
    the world burns? Could that pale poppy tall poppy
have unfurled her petals in this glittering dust?   Will   pour
ashes   gold-glinting hair   when   I   under the black
earth? Though
    not exactly tender-ankled

C went to the lavatories to see if B was there, but the cubicles were all empty. B's coat was still hanging up, her scarf and hat. Encouraged, C hurried back to B's

    ivy sprouted behind her and dewy petals fell
on the steps as B ran   trailing clouds of glory   carries
the potted grass as an offering   her perfumed foot
the dewy petals flushed from blush to ruby
        hoof-beats on the bare stair   hawthorn and
ash pressed her passing skin   silver apples tumbling
            rowan berries crushed

    hurried back to B's desk and saw, with a rush of relief as clear and dousing as a spring, that B's bag was still there. No-one would go

phone
spectacles testicles wallet and watch
passport money tickets door-key and coins
weapons

would go without their bag, you'd be lost without it. C felt younger, lighter. She re-joined the group that was still waiting for the two editors and now also for one of the clerks, confident that B would join them later.

Rob takes advantage   always dragging
B into stuff that should be his job   he's a
but they all are really, management

would join them later. Finally, the three wanderers returned, and the group clattered out into the foyer, to wait for

silver apples and nine bean rows lining
the unpainted stair-well   glimpsed
colour   green hare   ox   sapphire   boar
in wood   oak   bog oak   ivory
water babbles coldly round golden
apples   ivy grinds her desk to dust   mask falls ringing
and smashing   suit trails   buttons
hooves and bare feet ringing down the back stairs

to wait for the lift. C stepped into the

exactly like her handwriting that
sort of   formed not individual not expressive
legible though

into the lift last, and pressed the key for the ground floor. The lift was crowded, so she stood at the front, so people would not

she hardly wrote poetry at work, who would
memory exercise? Something like that? Should have
kept it just in
sure she'll be back shortly, why am I

        people would not wonder why she kept her eyes shut. The pressure of bodies against her back was repellent, the heat nauseating. C dreaded these moments of the day. Crowded trains, crowded trams, she would rather a pit of snakes, the slicing fang, the chill invasion by poison of the blood. Not the death, of course, annihilation, and

what was the start? The   was in skin?
Body? Skin as smooth as hyacinths

        annihilation, and the doors of the lift hissed as they opened. C surged out, tapping her card against the reader, and waiting

fruitless blossom   apples
spin, was it, spiral? Twirl? Memory's shot since

        reader, and waiting for the group to gather. The fire-door opened, but it was just the three from the editorial suite, whose days were driven by the software strapped to their arms, telling them how many steps they had taken during the day, giving them little

black earth, the birds fall and the stars are quenched.
sounds like a translation what was the fucking
point of all those years all that debt and now this
you're sold a pup from the day you're born

        giving them little jolts when they had been sitting down too long. C went and stood by the door, waiting. The fog had returned and gauzy wisps flickered by the windows when the

outside door flickered open, which it did, with the predict-
ability of a bored dog, at every passer-by. The day was on the
cusp of evening, when everything looked blue and violet, dark
but as though it had come from a long way off, and had faded
in transit. Standing, not thinking of anything

such a weird thing   exactly like cymbals,
smaller ones, finger-bells, whatever they're called

not thinking of anything but the pleasure
that awaited her when the day was at last over and she could
turn out the light on the whole fandangle, C looked at litter
fluttering. The evening was absolutely windless, so the bags
and bits of broken things were trying to reach escape velocity
by throwing themselves under the wheels of cars. The foyer
was wide and bright and tiled. The Eco-Committee—known
without affection as the Hobbits—had tried to persuade
management to get a living wall, but it had been too expensive,
so instead they had installed a

draught from the door, maybe? Something
is rustling

installed a number of large pot-plants, with
leaves so glossy

grating, even, rustling, or the trees outside
stunted things

so glossy they might be mistaken for plastic. The pots
looked well, and took away a little of the sterility that the anonymous artwork had instilled, by looking so very much like the
safe decisions of a committee. The little group bound for the
pub had reached capacity and approached the door, the card-
reader beeping rhythmically.

The fog was very thick and even the newest cohort, most likely to buck away like calves the moment they were off the clock, checked their stride for fear of crashing into something. The pavements were almost empty, the streets too. C looked at her watch several times, to make sure that there had not been some mistake, to make sure that it really was time to go home, rush-hour. She made a vague, and, later, unconvincing, association in her mind between the dense fog and the lack of noise. She walked near the back of the group, keeping company with one of the technicians, chatting amiably about bedding-plants and the union meeting, until something, or some gust of wind, rushed by and flared out the skirt of her coat. C and the technician stopped, and looked behind them, back up the street to the junction with the city's main drag. The fog was low and heavy, but above the buildings, fireworks had exploded, and the sky was sequinned with falling colours.

Watching the faded red and orange scintillate against the grey, smoky sky, C realized with a distinct shock that B would not return. Everything would be left as it was, bag and all.

"Is it me," said the technician, "Or are there an *awful* lot of dogs out tonight?"

No-one else seemed to notice. There were cats, too, sashaying and slinking while the dogs trotted about with the air of having places to go, and posts to piss on. Looking across the street, a tree seemed backlit against the murky fog, and along its amputated branches perched a clustering of birds, like tombstones or a wreath of studs around the bare tree-crown.

"They're parakeets," said a new voice beside her, "Long-escaped."

C blinked, unable to answer for several seconds. Then the binding in her brain released—an unexpected statement made by an unknown person had been too much, but now she recognized the face, looking out from between a violet hat and a corn-yellow scarf. C bought her sandwiches in the same shop every day.

"They look heraldic," she said, "Falcons in hoods."

"Happens oftener than you might think," said the woman, and her eyes crinkled because she was smiling under her scarf, "See you tomorrow, Wholemeal, Pickles, and Cheese."

The lights in the windows of the pub were blurred. C hoped

Despite what they say
they'll say anything, bosses, to gaslight you, make you think
> *but it's all rhetoric, all*
whatever guff they'll come out with now, about invaluable presence on the team,

> > > > > > > C hoped

it would not be too crowded. She hated a crowded pub, places people said were *great craic*. Nowhere to sit, unable

And people believe it, too
> *lynchpins, they think, even cogs in the machine*
maybe small and anonymous but necessary, that's the thing. People need meaning or they run amok

> > > > > to sit, unable to hear any-thing. This one was a bit down a side-street, no placards outside. Maybe it would do, since she had to be there.

So what they will say when B doesn't
> *but the truth will be that the office will do without B as a tree does without a plucked apple*

They were almost invisible to the shrouded city, sequinned as it was; now the city having been fuzzily awake, was falling back asleep under the fog, the foggy livid sky, fog blurring its details, everything hidden, then looming. The path revealed itself in stages, coyly revealing a curve round an hotel here, a flank past a chain of small, local shops there. Without seeing much beyond a couple of anonymous metres, C did not know how close they were to the side-road, without even the diminishing murmur of traffic to guide her, and no memory, she had never visited this pub. Here and there the street-lights were on, not so much shining as glistening.

The roots had overturned the slabs of concrete, so the foot-path rose up and then crumbled, and C stumbled, grabbing a branch for balance. Some birds flew up and out, scattered like they were shot from a gun. Slim, glittering birds. Twilight-coloured. Starlings, maybe.

Every minor thing that was visible through this tissue of seeping night seemed significant. The twilight world on display against an oyster-coloured fog

where is that line from? Some kid's book. Oyster-coloured fog.

forgetting of course that twilight bookends the day, twi-evening, twi-morning. Twixt.

…coloured fog

Necrologue

Someone is waiting for me to die. Me. Maybe. The priest's vestments are thick again, they've abandoned the modern materials, the modern's ceased to be. It's linen now, thick linen, thick like it was quilted. Though my eyes are half shut I can see the seams. It looks grey. It reminds me of something. A picture. Only it was a woman in it. Not a man. This priest is a man. Bastard.

They are snuffling at the end of my bed, snuffling like pigs, their eyes full of truffles and tears. They are looking for some sign from me. A raised hand to show that I want his blessing. All I want is to pick my nose but a raised finger would make them pounce. The gods have spoken, I can hear the squawking cry, anoint him. Anoint him.

Anoint me arse. Fuck off.

The priest moves closer. I can feel his hot breath on my cheek, his stubble brushes my cheek. He moves away and I see that a flake of my flesh has scraped away and dangles from the black hair. He has murmured something to me and his eye flicks sideways, I am half dead but I see the rhomboid reflection of the far way window in his eye, a pane of white over the blackness of his pupil. He glanced at me and I knew he didn't like me. I was an awkward bugger, he knew that, he knew I would hold out and that there'd be nothing in it for him, not even a shilling at the gate of heaven.

It was that that did it for me. Knowing the priest didn't like me, I mean. I was too happy to die then. Fuck the lot of them. I thought I would not be able to do it, and that I would die trying. Which is why I did it, really. I thought I knew what would happen. But it didn't. Anyway, what I did was this: I raised myself first up onto my elbows, the joints snapping and popping moistly.

"Has he seen a vision? Is it a vision?"

Some old bitch was bundled up in the corner, some ancient old slag who could function as nothing any longer except as a prayer-raiser, earning a miserable existence at the foot of death-beds.

"No," said the priest sharply. No one as bedevilled as me would have a vision. The angels did not descend from the seventh sphere for cussed bastards like me. No, they didn't.

I couldn't speak, my throat was parched and full of painful cracks that throbbed beautifully when a meagre stream of water covered them. My lips were swollen. The insides, now brightly pink and slick, puffed out over the thin, stretched band of the outer lip. Minute flakes of skin clung and fell, and the corners were blocked with a shockingly white scurf. I don't know who it was, in their wisdom, who strategically placed the mirror so that anyone pushing themselves upwards with their hands and glancing, as we do instinctively, towards the window, towards a means of egress, could see themselves. Perhaps they feared I might do it, that I might start to struggle back from the gateway into the Valley of Death, and they thought to scare me into the arms of the Prime Mover by letting me see the sight of myself. I had tramped the world over and dragged my banded rags through every city and hellhole, I had slept nights in sewers and at the last rattle of brutal sicknesses, and they thought to scare me into faith by my reflection in a polished glass.

Mind you, I look at myself now and I think perhaps they had a point.

The mirror is badly polished, at that, but I see clearly what it is that they have had to look at this last week and for a nano-second I feel a fleeting pity for them. They don't know what to say. I brought back my own sickness from the filthy heathen countries I chose to visit, so they should be able to happily wash their hands of me and leave me to die, and to descend, as they believe I should, to the First Sphere. But I stomped from country to country, growling and shouting, for what they also believe is a noble cause. I had the Necrologue.

The realization of the inevitable discomfort of that particular cleft stick pleases me and gives me enough strength to continue my journey into the vertical.

The greatest distance I travelled was into the East, out where the Crusades had been fought millennia ago. It would hardly be the death of me to run out into the garden but the fact of the matter is that I hoped it would. I wanted them to have to chase my corpse. Dead man running.

I was used to running. I had lived my life almost always in sewers, that is how I got from country to country. The whole world was reduced to that but we didn't say so. No, we pretended. And that was how I survived. Night after black night, cities full of people all staring at the stars—*what are they saying now? Are we safe yet?* They lay on the mountains, on the hills and on the turrets. I sneaked below them, gathering the names and adding them to my list.

Now any of you lazy bastards who have bothered to read any of your recent history, any of you who have the faintest interest in why it is the world seems to be going down the sink hole and doing its best to turn itself into an arse hole will have missed reading about the disappearance of the Emperor of Never. The blistering heat flashing like the wrath of the Angel from the helmets of the men, the swirling clouds of red dust in the brittle desert heat and the impatient hooves of the stallions, not a cliché left unchewed by every hack journalist around and many of the serious faces from the quality newspapers, the kind of newspapers that your budgie wouldn't be ashamed to see on the floor of his cage. The battle, the steel the shouts of the fighters and the screams of frightened horses and then, abruptly, the end. They were gone.

The journalists stood, puzzled, on the ends of phones in their sweating hotels, looking into the old-fashioned receivers as though the smooth metal would tell them something. Bar owners and taxi drivers, leaning their elbows on their counters or glancing in the rear-view mirror at their trapped audience, choking off into silence, predictions left unmade, crafty interpretations exposed and naked and false. People stood in the streets looking at each other, at the white walls, then up at the shield-blue sky like it would tell them something. There was a second in the whole world into which anything could have fallen. And the fucking Angels got there first, fuck them from a height. Into the pre-natal silence from which anything could have come—a symphony, Venus rising, a magical tree—a caterwaul went up and the bastard Angelites claimed this moment of birth for themselves. This was proof, they said, of what they had always maintained, that the ancient bands round the earth were true, spirits and humours and ideals and what have you floating serenely between them, and a deputation of Angels to make sure each band was ticking over. All as you might imagine, these Angels, dream-coloured wings and long dresses and smug smiles you want to smack off their faces.

After everything else they'd all been through it was not surprising that people flocked to this. My grandfather had been in the desert at that battle. Being the low scum that we were he wasn't on a shining stallion or encased in silver armour. He had not come of the right stock for that bright history. He was on the ground dodging and running and shitting himself, stabbing here, biting there, hoping he didn't maim or kill the wrong person. When he didn't come back to his factory-work lifestyle my grandmother's grief drove her into the ethereal wings of the angels and we became the most viciously Angelite family for miles.

That priest waving angrily out the window at me is tired, the old prick. He can't give up. He has to be the stony face that does not hear the insult or feel the missile. They wear all the vestments that they used to clear a path through the scavenging, oily clothed street urchins in the cities when the priests were ascendant and though the urchins now include the unskilled but savage priests who ran away, some, stubborn, stupid, hand-washed the heavy grey skirts and ironed the length of surplice in shabby rooms. Bastard. Everywhere you go now you cannot escape the afterlife, the pride in the faces of people who have winkled the reality out from behind the merely manifest, you can dispute it and you will hear happy talk of wheels and everything being one but you see a glitter in an eye, a hidden eye where before it had only been a dark corner, a sideways movement away in a tavern.

I went to the desert. I went where he disappeared. The last sight of my grandfather. You'd disappear too, if the place was rotten with vast underground caverns, big tunnels joining them up. I don't know what they were. They used to say there were trains ran in tunnels, but who knows what that looked like? I did. I saw maps, you see. No one else was allowed see maps but a Necrologue, that was different, I had to see them, see? Mincy old fuckers couldn't not let such a holy one not see where to hell they were going. I saw the maps from years ago and the straight lines and the projections. That would have explained the iron stairs.

I knew what would happen if I said anything about it. Some years ago, some poor bollocks was digging up his land, whether he expected to find a mine of gold or he was just wanting to plant one bastard of a crop, he dug and dug and his sons dug and his neighbours dug and they found just such a stairs. He, having some shred of sense left despite the unveiled sun and thunderous past, bethought himself of these shreds of history, but no. These were, it was announced, a sign that arrogant ancestors had tried to build a stairway through the Angelic Spheres. I haven't heard anything that stupid since the Tower of Babel.

Anyway they invented a whole story about it, the civilization, what it looked like, what those hubristic forebears had looked like and their long fanatical eyes yearning to see the faces of the Angels. And the poor dick with the shovel? Well. One of life's little mysteries, what happened to him. But sitting in the desert I knew what I was looking at. I took my own little shovel, with a cherry-wood handle, and I dug. There was no one to see me but vultures. Just enough to let me in and to see the irregular serrated iron step, a tattered remnant of bridle, the moonlight gleam of the first skull. Collapse and landslide. Angels, my arse.

There is sand under my feet now. It is a dark night and very very cool, almost solid, cool and reassuring. There are no clouds. The moon is stripped and shadowless, the stars like perfect thoughts. There is a garden, a little border garden. It has cool leafed flowers with petals with colours like jellybeans. Jellybean. Now there's a word. I've never eaten a jellybean—though I have eaten flowers, when things got rough—but I know what they look like. The house is a shadow behind me, blurred edges, cloth-filtered lights. My knees are shaking, they look enormous in my scrawny legs. The skin is so dry and lined I look like a fossil. A dreadful cackle emerges from my lips and I realize I have laughed. That thought makes me laugh again. A legend will start if I don't stop. I am sick with tiredness. I wonder will I break anything if I sit down. Fuck it, I'm practically dead, what can happen? I creak down and sit. The grass is cold under me but it instantly warms to me. Feebly my toes flick the sand.

I had to stay a while in a monastery on my way back from the desert. It was like a different world, high wet wind and cliffs safe from landslide because they had been so stripped to the heart rock there was nothing left to fall. The men and women in their black gowns with the strange little coloured beads around their wrists. They had a huge dinner when I was there and they were very polite about not letting me near the table until I had washed. For fuck sake I had had to crawl through a sewer on three occasions on the way back and even without the shite of a city clinging to me, walking and sweating and never being able to wipe my arse would make anyone smell. But they chucked me into a big ceramic bath that was full of red water and leaves, and enough foam to cover my modesty as well as wash me and this bustley woman monk gave me a good scrubbing. I grinned up at her and she just rolled her eyes, she'd probably seen better and been getting it oftener than me. She kept her beads about her wrist. They were a furry sort of red colour, and they smelled sweet. I caught her wrist and grabbed the beads and sniffed them. I looked at her.

"Rosewood," she said.

A little band of the beautiful beads like a bracelet on her wrist.

"And you'll pray for the people who can't eat," I said, in a sing song voice, "On your little rosewood beads."

"Fuck you," said the monk and shoved my head under the water to apply the scrubbing brush to my hair. When I was out of the bath and drying on the mat she looked quite surprised, as though she hadn't expected under all the shite and the clothes so old they had to be peeled off me like paper that there would be anything worth looking at. Mind you, she scrubbed so hard she could have brought a diamond out of granite. She smiled at me, and I flashed her but she just went pink and raised her eyebrows nonchalantly.

The dining hall was a marvel to behold, with a vaulted ceiling and tall windows with narrow panes of glass. There were tables all along the sides and sloped black shapes ducking towards their plates, leaning back to spit out gristle, standing up to grab the salt or punch their neighbour. At the far end was the nobs' table, a gem-eyed man with a beard, a boy with a face like thin alabaster. Here, I ate. We didn't speak, I just ate for all the days to come when I would find no food. And afterwards I had to earn my keep. Everyone was silent. I walked into the sunken bit of the floor, shaped like a horseshoe only without the bits of shit and people's bones stuck on. I dragged my bag behind me as though it weighed like the world, which it did, it was full of dead people.

I looked round me solemnly, trying to keep with the mood, but I was reckless and that alarmed me, something was running through me like an intoxicant and I feared it was the desire to shock. I unfurled my life's work, paper ran on for miles. I looked round and everyone was silent. The gem-eyed man said,

"We have heard until June 7th of last year."

Hmm, I wondered, who told them that much? Fuckers.

I filled my belly with wind and my voice blew out like a trumpet.

"*Manger Dorset,*" I bellowed, "*Trampled.*"

"*Ram Dolly. Appendicitis.*"

"*Nory Pepper. Choked on vomit. His own.*"

"*Ittie Lamplaz. Died of being aged 102.*"

"*Felly Rubble. Blood poisoning.*"

There was a rustle of arses in seats and the breathing changed. They were getting sucked in by the words and waited, in hope with a tiny crumb of watered-out fear, that they would hear a name they knew.

"*Yelk Mann. Drowned.*"

"*Pqvta Mann. Also Drowned.*"

"*Lackey Pard. Crushed by landslide.*"

"*Edoll Tayama. Committed suicide by means of hanging.*"

"*Says Timmer. Bled to death after amputation of leg.*"

Usually I stood in one place when I read the chosen section of the Necrologue. That way if anyone couldn't hear me they just had to shout and I would know where to move. But that fuck-you-all feeling was rippling under my skin and there was nothing I could do but scratch it. I walked towards the pit.

"*Tarette June. Stillborn.*"

They thought they were hearing the population of heaven. This was a personal introduction to the choirs of Angels—Archangel Gabriel, this is the Abbot Smalls. Pleased to meet you. Likewise, I'm sure.

"Garganta Smalls. Kicked by his horse."

I was viewed as a sort of escort agency of the afterlife. They heard the names, they suddenly knew the Spheres of the Immortals, did they, and the names gave them protection from being the next one like poor *Raman Korik Influenza*. They made me laugh and made me so angry I could have killed them all, with one great roar, one great thunderous explosion of vengeance. There was nothing in this except the poor sons of whores who had died. That was the only reason I did this insane job. There would be these irrefutable double-facts; these people had lived, these people had died. The world would not whirl on into a tangled future without there being the reminder that *Bail Newfork* lived and died from *Eating fermented berries*. Poor little cow. She'd only been three. That is what eventually did for me. Not the realization that I did not believe in the Spheres, in the Gods of the Spheres, which I had been taught to revere for all of my life. It was the realization that I did not believe that what I did had any point. Where are these names going to go? I had not realized that I needed eternity.

They said that thousands and thousands of years ago there lived people who were giants and strong, and who had been born from the heads of eagles. They had circular cities and they travelled all around the world and when they died they became petrified, their apotheosis the transformation into huge statues made of polished marble. Now and then, as the countries of the world tossed and split and fell in upon themselves, parts of this ancient life were revealed back to us. An upraised arm here, a hand modestly covering an imposs-ible nipple, the foundations of a building to give guidance to our modern fools trying to raise a building that won't fall down at the first fart. The monastery where I was staying had been one such place, it had found the circular origins of a long gone city, but the bit that they had got, though useful, was not perhaps what the Abbot would have chosen. There was no question but that cities have always been built on shit and that the means of tidying the effluvia of the citizens is a clue to the state of the state. That ancient culture had some nifty shite arena. Right in the middle of the hall was the crumbled semi-circle of stone baked under a remembered sun. Dusty and bits still crumbling so the monks would get up with grit and buttons of stone embedded in their buttocks. A little step for your feet while you sat and a bottomless seat where you could sit and chat while you strained.

"*Paritty Gull,*" I intoned, pacing slowly forward, "*Alcohol poisoning.*"

"*Nate Bloogar. Choked on a fishbone.*"

I stepped down into the sunken arena and I could hear them shifting in their seats, some unable to hear, some being put in mind by my position of the turmoil in their guts, clamouring to get out.

"*Avvid Lore. Car crash.*"

"*Weston Fish. Leukaemia.*"

My flesh thrilled to the unmistakable gasp that sounded; it slipped out through unprepared throats. Now that the rosy-titted monk had scrubbed away the clothes that had been growing on me the last years, the robe, butter yellow, slid briskly up my legs and I bunched it, like a wedding train you see in ancient old paintings of certain ceremonies, over my arm.

"*Dassy Roy. Race Attack—kicked to death.*"

"*Juntie Kracker. AIDS.*"

The abbot, gem-eyes gaping and his dark cheek lumpy with blood, was facing the smooth moon of my arse, then the dark curled silk in front, atop my long brown legs, as I turned, very slowly, reading.

"*Tamede Almata. Dehydration in a detention centre.*"

"Dot Commis. Lung Canker."

I sat down and wriggled to settle myself in. No one on the list yet died of having a shit in public so I settled in and let rip.

I didn't really think I'd last the night and I was right. The monk who washed me brought me to the square white room which they had set aside for me, washed and aired as soon as they knew that the Necrologue would be coming their way. They had to add their names to my list, which the abbot, killing himself to pretend he couldn't see me wiping my arse with my free hand, read out the names and the causes of death for me to scratch on to the paper after poor *Halana Pae* who had been snuffed out by *making too many shoes.*

"Brother Carmatel," said the abbot through gritted teeth, *"Drug overdose."*

I knew, I could see in his eyes, he was struggling with an ultimatum he did not dare to give to god. *Strike this cunt, this son of a bitch dead or I will never believe again.*

"Sister Latam. Pernicious Anaemia."

Give me another Necrologue that I may be spared entrusting the brethren's names to this.

I smirked as I left the room but I already had an eye to the narrow chute down to the kitchens where I knew I could land back into a midden heap, a favourite haunt of mine. The monk with the rosewood beads showed me the room and shut the window while I slithered out of the yellow robe and sat cross legged and titty naked on the bed. She laughed, and I looked at my watch.

"I washed my hands and everything," I said, "And I have probably half an hour before they come to boot my well-observed arse out of the window."

It only took twenty minutes and she seemed pleased and I was nicely set up to go creeping around the intestines of the monastery, to go crawling out of the cloaca of the abbot's home. Well fed, well watered and well laid. What more was there to want?

I can't remember her face now. All I can remember is the raspberry shade of her mouth and the way she laughed. Her hair was like silk.

I can see them in the lighted window. They are debating whether they should come down for me. Even at this distance I can see the look of horror on the face of the old bitch the prayer-raiser, the resentment on the face of the priest. He no more wants to come anywhere near me, wouldn't piss on me if he could avoid it. The old biddy is terrified and frosts it with sanctimonious rolling of the eye. The others, the washers, the carriers, the lifters, they are weak in expression and they look mulish. They think the priest has to be immune, *no better than them fuckers the Angelites if he's not immune*. But the poor bollocks doesn't know what it is I have. The whites of his eyes show at the possibility that he might have to die of the breath of a shitty rag like me. He would have been astounded, I was astounded, to know of the sumptuous, satin lined place in which I contracted it. Whatever the fuck it is.

It isn't what they had in the court, that's for sure. The prince was flailing; his father was failing upstairs, his life seeping away, pushed out by the hardened residue of a life spent fucking the parlour maids, the prince was in charge. Powerful and stupid, his weak head grew merely hot and full of wind when faced with any problem; faced with an epidemic he could hardly stand up. He stayed in his breakfast room all day eating peaches and only sometimes he had the courage, silk wrapped over his face, to flee across the courtyard to the stables where his chestnut would bear him away and the stable hands may or may not be alive when they got back. The prince had screamed for blessings from the Abbey and the abbot, who did not like the earthly princes at all, slyly kneaded his hands and mournfully told the prince that there was at least a Necrologue in the vicinity, if not a cure.

So I was dragged in from the highway, stumbling and hurrying with a tattered yellow gown and the bones of the dead on my back. I scribbled the names on the paper as fast as I could; I became impatient with the *cause of death unknown.* It should bloody be known. It's the only thing we do. So I went and had a look at them. It is not often I had occasion to praise the country of my birth but somehow this court had managed to contract a virus common where I was brought up. They'd never seen it before and had no clue what they should do about it. The fever, the delirium, the skin colour, all left the doctors scratching their scabby heads and lost ones wailing at the back walls near the pits. It was really quite easy.

"A little of this," I said, "And a little of this, a pinch of that, a spoonful of that one over there and a few drops of the hard stuff to make it less revolting—for fuck sake don't spit it out you stupid wanker."

The prince was instantly in love with me. The king, when he heard, was so grateful he would have let me suck him but I said I could only chew so we left it at that. The communal fevers dissipated, the heat of fear and sickness had gone. I was allowed to stay.

She was curled up by the redcurrant bushes when I saw her. A comma of a woman in a swathe of tangerine silk, her bare feet turned towards me, her face turned east. The sun fell in little drops on her jewellery. She was not doing anything, just looking. In front of her were patterns that even I saw instantly. The rounded phlox of darkness in the centre of the bushes, the stark sap green leaves, the perfect, luminescent red globes hanging perfectly still from the brown stems. She was being perfect, doing nothing. I stood still, looking at her, watching the way the cloth and her skin and her jewellery absorbed the light and the sun and made the air look richer for it. I knew, or at least I guessed that she was one of the king's concubines, but she turned around and looked at me and smiled and I knew instantly that she might have been procured for that reason but that the king had never laid a hand on her. With an elegance that made me want to dance she turned around so she was still coiled but facing me. The king's cock would have fallen off in terror if he had tried to make it stand up to her. I knew it for a fact. Mine nearly did and I didn't even have one.

She was the blackest person I had ever seen, so black she was almost violet, so black her white teeth, her tawny palms came as a shock, and she was a giant, she must have been over seven feet tall. But it was neither her colour in a milky, pink-and-yellow country nor her size that made her so terrifying. It was her eyes. She looked at you and you wanted to roll over to her like a croquet ball. Wrap yourself up in pretty paper with a bow in her favourite colour and hope she would unwrap you. Put your viscera on a plate and see if it entertained her. She smiled at me and I subsided like a ghost when the child runs out from under the sheet.

I could never do it with her. I was certain of that. I helped her pick flowers for the staff quarters, and I helped her clean the swans' lake and I helped her wash the dogs and groom the horses. I sat with her once while she bathed. The bath was big and square, a ceramic bath, white, with little flattened bits for the honey soap. The tiles around it were also square and white but they had red splashes on them, like a curl of red smoke in hardened glass. She spoke to me gently and easily. She spoke everyone's language, seven or ten languages and people came to her to translate and she would do it, always the same with everyone. Letters of diplomacy for the ministers, letters from the mothers of the ten year old apprentice gardeners, re-read in their language by her gentle, easy voice. The water in her bath was green from the scented pellets she put into it, and white petals floated. She talked to me and I said something that made her laugh, she lay back and laughed a chuckly sort of delighted laugh and lifted her legs up, paddling her feet on the surface of the water like she was walking on it. She kicked her feet up and I wanted nothing more, ever, not a single other thing in the world but her clean legs with rivulets of water running down and the plashing noise of her feet, and the shapes she made on the tiles and the water.

But then of course I got sick and I had to go. Whatever my country gave them that they could not cure, they had their own medical peculiarities. They had germs of their own, the bastards, at the mention of which everyone looked wide eyed and innocent. They had been immune to it for so long that no one got ill any more. Even if I had given it to her she would not even have noticed. And they were all very sorry but they couldn't fucking couldn't cure me when I started to die.

"Why do you not believe in the Angels, the god of the spheres?" she asked. I never asked her name because I never wanted to add it to the Necrologue.

I told her. I have never told anyone else.

I had been brought up from a child with one of those fucking angels hovering at my shoulder. I couldn't piss without them knowing about it. But I believed and I said what I was told to say and I believed what I was told to believe. We no longer had any reasons for anything, no coherence against the chaos, no thread to bring us from the monster's cave into the light of civilization. We deduced, from what we had experienced, the real causes for things and on what seemed apparent, and the strength of our emotions and what seemed to keep us safe. It was less that I believed, and more that I did not *not* believe, until when I was eleven, I was struck by lightning. And I survived, but nothing else did. The jolt did not shatter me or snap my bones apart but when we were certain I was still alive and when that apocalyptic intrusion from the Spheres into my world became part of my history, rather than I part of its, everything had snapped apart. What had happened to me had not killed me, as I would have expected. I was not different as a result of it, as I had expected. It had happened for its own reason and it had nothing to do with the mysterious and esoteric lines and tangled threads with which we had attempted to map the idea of it before it had even happened. It was a different colour, when it happened, a different smell, a different everything. Like the first time you drink or get high or make love. Never what you imagine, good bad or ugly but never what you thought it would be and never, ever, conceivably, any other way. So don't tell me about angels. Even if they existed we would know nothing of them. Wouldn't recognize them. Cocooned by the timorous pictures we would draw and the protective mesh of notion, expectation that would rip apart at the first brush of the actual. Don't fucking tell me about fucking angels.

I had meant to tell her quietly and gently as she spoke to me but I was pacing up and down over the stone by the time I had finished. I knew I was sick then, too, and that I would have to go so I cared even less than I did by the time I was twelve. We were in what I knew had been an old church, a mega church, high almost as the sky because the spire was left though bits of the walls had fallen out the coloured glass was still there. Thin, impossibly thin columns swooped into arches and clustered together like pagan fists in the centre. There was a raised table with steps up to it, and a stone, a big stone slab. From there we could see right back into the back of the church, past the sapling forest of columns, to the four tall windows with tiny rectangles of coloured glass. I paced as I spoke and I felt as full of electricity as if I had been struck again. She was sitting on the white slab. She was wearing green and on her arms she wore bands of jade and silver. I stared at her and I can recall very little else. Not because I don't remember what happened, but because I never really knew. I was enveloped by her. Green silk and gold thread that straggled from the edge of the cloth, bloomy grape skin, her white teeth, her eyes that could redirect towards her everything about another person, her hands with the most delicate, elegant bones, the tawny palms, irrefutable woman, unquestionable solidity, flashes of copper, of apricot, of coral and shell pink when she smiled and made me fall to pieces that she was pleased, of rose and poppies with dark hearts. And somewhere in all of this bobbed I, ginger-topped snuff-coloured streak and there was not a single fucker in the world better than me because I made her smile and she had wanted me.

The night is very dark now. I had always said my last act would be to write my own name in the Necrologue. I am not going to. I do not, now, know, whether to scream till I bleed, or just sit, quietly, looking at the petals that are turning black with night, becoming secrets that I might have unfurled but have not.

Like scabs they all fall away. The spheres of heaven, the circles of hell, the world ceiling and wall in symbol. We stand in a carnival hall, trick mirrors and sly hands tilting them this way and that. Words writ large, the whole bag of bones and knives rattled in our ears so we can't hear and barely tell where we stop and that which we fear begins. I do not know how many years I have lived. Thirty? Forty? And in all that time I never seen eternity. I yelled in triumph that I have not been fooled, I see the warp in the glass, the fake limb hidden in the jacket, marked cards, loaded dice, lies, innocent faces, fucking lies. I stagger under the silence.

The sky is black and full of stars. If I close my eyes I can hear the sea, the memory of the sea. Shells. Fossils in a grey mountain. I will die here, and for the first time that I recall, I do this not because *they don't want me to*. Because I want to. I sit in eternity and am briefly a god. For me to go to my grave with my knowledge of the cracks beneath the plaster has not been enough, and it is too late, now, to go with anything else. The dark is smooth like a jelly, her touch, my life, distilled into one breath. And I am about to die. *Fuck.*

Fleeting Fluctuation in Disorder

IN THE MONTH that I have worked here, my sensitivity to the room's mood had built up, or, conversely, worn away, so that the slightest shift of the thin winter sun rang, like a breath on an exposed nerve. Every day had that indefinable moment when it is done and the evening gathers, twilight draws in, and so the night. In spaces such as these exhibition rooms, with everything measured to the millimetre, and the labels to the last word, the indefinable moment of transition is pushed to centre-stage. Twilight in the spotlight. This day was the day, D-day, the last job day.

Over and back over and back pacing the room in soundless shoes and smiling. Keeping an eye. Over and back. Murmured answer a whispered question, nodding. The Ladies?—down the hall to the right. The restaurant already, you greedy little beggar? Through the door at the top of the room. Over and back over and back. The capillary motion of daylight across the pristine glass of the exhibition cases marking the progress of today towards its catalytic hour.

The morning had been bright, positively glowing, the sort of magnificent winter sun that makes even this island bewitching. The day declines quickly at this time of year, and the afternoon was misty, and glistening with sea-fret, grey but a grey peculiar to this place, like a pearl that is in some manner dead. Over and back. Yes, they do sell reproductions of the map in the gift-shop. Over and back. Yes, they do sell miniature models of the stuffed wildlife on display. Over and back. Everyone wanted the gift-shop—even me, in a manner of speaking. The key to the sweetshop, the code to open the storage bay, and Fann's list in my pocket. Over and back.

We had been busy today. The island is—all the islands in

this archipelago are—long deserted but some crony of the Premier got millions to build bridges to the island; tourists, they said. For those of us unenchanted by cuddy-duck or kittiwake there is Christenson House and its museum, the target of today's visitors from one of the coastal public schools. This was usual, apparently, in the week before their mid-term break. That none of them had been sea-sick was less usual, another attendant had told me bitterly at coffee-break. I could hear the teenagers progress between the exhibition cases in the eastern room

> it's so tiny! Oh my god,   That looks like real ivory, I know 'cos my uncle is like   I just…can't   believe the size of   I have to have it,   it's the cutest thing ever

and the noise rolled between exhibition cases and the surly silences of the goths, and the emos who are unimpressed with everything, even the first edition of *Frankenstein*, even the glass cases displaying love-tokens—most made of hair—through the ages.

Sound and silence do not mix here.

The enhanced reactions of the teenagers tumble and ring on the polished stone floor in the same way that their darkening shadows flash on the stone walls or blear a window—their progress is brief and traceless. There was a child in the charge of an adult yesterday, they huddled in emerald corduroy coats over every case in the Early Ceramics Room, their whispers intense. In the Medical Room this morning, a Louis Vuitton parent loudly whispered to their juniors that these bits of plasticized nervous systems, these models in age-translucent wax of eviscerated women with their faces modestly turned away, were just like the pictures in Daddy's study, and weren't they *interesting*? The parent curdled equally at both the ardent daughter and the repulsed son. Nothing changed the silence, which endured the noise, and then remained as the waves and billows retreated.

Silence was an essential property of the museum. That was the difference. The ringing or murmuring or bullying, the running or jostling footfalls, fluttering scarves, the clatter of cutlery and crockery on crockery, all accidentals, all transient properties fading in their hour.

I believe silence to be an essential property of my room, too. It is half-revealed, as the room is half-finished, and waiting to emerge. I have imagined this room always as silent, I realize, as I pace towards the exit, jerk my chin sympathetically at the wind-whipped duty-guard, and pace back. It has been in my head these twenty years, this room; elegant, proportionate, with, as you might say, beautiful bones. It is a sanctuary. Naturally, it is silent.

Over and back. Patience was difficult today.

Finally, advent. I wasn't even looking at the window, and I could tell.

It happens when the last smear of sun slips its hold on the windowsill. The temperature drops. But what really changes is tension. Not in a psychological sense, no. These curated spaces are ordered and harmonious, and they breed quietude. It is not relaxation but adjustment. The dissolution of the light into grains acts as a tuning-fork or as a lead violin, to which keynote every voice and every instrument adjusts itself. Everything of the day—the over and back, the morning light, the dull afternoon sky, simmering bright water, the voices— everything thickens and can be lifted like a lactoderm and removed, at the right time. This happens every day and everywhere. But a museum, that takes the quotidian from its natural setting, heightens these things: change, and silence.

Time now. Time now, ladies and gentlemen. Finish up rinsing your young in culture. I have work to do.

Waiting, again, between the exhibition room and the storage bays that had been my target all this time.

Places like the vestibule are hangers-on in the ordered world of collections and exhibitions. By-blows, unacknowledged, with no function other than to join alien worlds together, and to cause unease. Christenson House had been remodelled so often that the vestibule separating the exhibition room from the storage bay has a beauty and elegance more proper to a public place, but it is a parasite, an unswept floor that can only live alongside a feast. Locked in the storage bay behind me were the sweepings of the museum's collection: new acquisitions in an uncatalogued limbo, old acquisitions too tattered or controversial for display. These places draw me.

The only job Fann ever offered me that I turned down was for a client looking for a work by an outsider artist called de Selby. It had turned up in some little local museum—Fann and his patronizing air-quotes—and I could have put it under my coat and walked out, unchallenged. But I liked places like that, former schoolhouses turned cultural centre. This place, Christenson House, with its declarations about how things were in the past. Full of the big stories. History writ large. The little museum, random as it was, was a collection of rumours by comparison, of gossip. I liked that thought. It had, I felt, resonance with my own situation. Head Curators glossing the stories of how the jewels and the hunted wildlife and all the rest of it got to be there, squinting over the documentation to prove the chains of custody, and leaving out the lionizing of slaughter and theft. I take things away, and sell them to Fann, and Fann sells them to his secretive contacts. His client gets something they really want. Fann gets money, and gets to spit in the eye of the "neo-liberal Philistine project managers hollowing out cultural resources and growing fat on their entrails". I get to build up, piece by glorious piece, my private room.

The door in the vestibule had a tiny squint of glass in it. I waited among the ruptured packing-boxes, and empty pedestals, and their shadows, while the anonymous pipes gurgled and hissed. The visitors had been herded from the rooms.

While I watched, the last orange coat and the last scarlet beret flared in the charcoal mouth of the exit and vanished. I took out the keys, and murmured the code.

That was, by my calculation, a day and a half ago.

The storage bay was passive to the point of hostility. Naturally, there were shelves, as predicted by the plan Fann had sketched. Each space marked off with a reference number, but the floor was not visible under its burden of history, while the shelves had great gaps between boxes and cases. The electric lights ran on a dedicated generator (Fann had told me) because the curators saved some pennies by turning off the electricity over holidays. The room's vestigial windows had been bricked up, but there were lights in every corner. Bright as it was, it had an uncomfortably refracted quality: glass cases reflected again and again in their opposite numbers, partially visible contents overlain with another and another. As soon as I stepped inside, I was uneasy.

There was a moment, though. A few seconds before I reached behind me and pulled shut the door. Nothing fancy, a familiar, plain few seconds of crystalline clarity that occur when the inevitable is revealed for what it is: a series of choices, each choice obscuring its opposite. It is not even a revelation of that obscured opposite. All that is illuminated is the fact that the plan is, not an inevitability, but a possibility, and subject to mutation. Nothing was beyond recall. I could reverse over the lintel, and phone a security guard to come back and let me out, tell some tale of a distracted search for house-keys. As to Fann, I had already decided that our business was concluded. I had planned to have his acquisitions delivered and my pay received, and afterward to have no contact with him at all. What did I need the money for, anyway?

That was the thought that galvanized me. My room, on which I had worked for years, was within a whisper of completion. I had never varied in my vision of it, not once, and not by so much as a tassel. To abort it now would, I realized with, yes, crystalline clarity, ruin everything. My first job for Fann had paid for the hand-made wallpaper, another had released me into an auction to bid pitilessly for the antique desk, and the lamps. Who would sweat for years to obtain, say, the Lewis Chessmen, and accept the loss of a queen for the sake of speed? Out of fear of a little disorder?

I shut the door behind me. I didn't check for a handle because—well, you don't think, do you?

When I shut the door, it was that word that struck me, disorder, and in striking, it dislodged from some fold of my brain the school-memory of a law of physics. All things, so I am led to believe, move from an ordered state to a disordered one. Which made this chaotic place more advanced than the impeccably curated space I had just left.

I ticked off from my list the specimens as I found them. In among the museum's passenger pigeons and the St Stephen's Island Wrens and Jamaican petrels crammed onto shelves and stacked on the floor, I found the hollow, dusty little exemplars of the buyers' parameters of covetousness: vermillion-winged this, ground-nesting that, puff-legged the other, in glass-fronted cases, dead and dusted for so long that the labels were ornate manuscripts, and it was almost a joy to rob them. I wondered if I should worry about tetanus. The dust from rusted locks was like a crust on my hands.

The great auk was not in a case, but on a table.

I have owned my apartment for many years, but never lived there, and will not until the last room is ready. There was no hurry—its refurbishment is a project that had its genesis a couple of decades ago. I was living in a city I could not bear, in order to be near—well, anyway. Every day I walked home from my loathsome job, and I passed a house, a detached house in the middle of a row. It had shutters in the windows, but they were almost never closed. At the risk of being spotted, and incurring an insufferable obligation to explain, I stopped as long as I could, so that I could imagine being in possession: those flawless dark-red walls, the aureoles of bright gold from the wall-mounted lights, the shelves of books and beautiful things, and the high-backed chair. Oh, the beautiful things.

The items for removal were set on a table, each one newly tagged with the coded reference we used for the clients. They were a faded crew, alright, fogged with dust, and their colours leached, some of the feathers distinctly nibbled. The auk was the largest. It had white patches at its eyes so it must have been killed in summer. I did not know how I knew that. I read the beautiful copper-plate script on its expansive label. The label told me that the bird was one of the last breeding pair killed on this island. When the egg they were incubating was smashed too, the auk became extinct. That was a moment, too, a couple of seconds at most. There is nothing in this museum that is a monument to that transformation from a world with auks to a world without auks.

The storage room being so much larger, and so much more chaotic than Fann's drawing had predicted, I took an unconscionable amount of time getting everything together. Come midnight, I was only two-thirds of the way through. In the same way that I had known without looking that the day had changed to evening, and so to closing time, I could tell without external reference the point at which I knew I would stay all night. So accustomed am I to the swift execution of the tasks, that for a long time I reassured myself that it was just taking a little longer. It was a delay to routine, not a new experience. The delay had its causes: the black lines and the red ink scribbles on Fann's drawing bore no relationship with the room or its contents. I had to move and replace a dozen specimens for each one I sought. Eventually, and in a single, perfect moment of realization, I saw that there was no delay. My being here at midnight had nothing to do with Fann's drawing or anything else. I merely had been creating excuses to disguise the true nature of events: the disintegration of a simple plan into the clumsy execution of disjoined tasks. It—the job—was not taking longer, it was merely taking its time. It would not happen tonight. That the door had no handle on the inside was too peculiar to worry about. Fann would be able to open the door from the outside. I would provision myself for the night, finish the job in the morning, and send Fann a text to explain.

The night spent in the storage room was inevitable, and silence was its essential property.

I don't sleep well at the best of times. Being in a sealed room on a cold night on a practically deserted island with no mobile phone coverage and several continents' worth of dead animals was not the best of times. Even for me. At least I did find a couple of blankets, the felted sort used by furniture removers, and quite a lot of packing-straw. The depth of night, when it came, was freezing. I sat up, huddled under the blankets, picturing material treats with which to reward myself on release, to distract me from the suddenly pressing material discomforts. I was grateful for the food, limited as it was to snacks that hikers carry, and more so for the bottle of water, and even more so for the fact that I unearthed a gallon jerry-can with a wide mouth. The kidneys only produce about a litre a day. Don't some people drink urine? Someone else found a way to power batteries with it. I had no such ambitions, was just hoping not to spill any that could be analysed for DNA. Or start to smell before I got out. I turned out most of the lights, made myself comfortable so as to encourage sleep. My eyes adjusted to the dark, and without meaning to, I glanced around. The few lights I had left on were still glinting on the powdery eyes of the specimens. The auk stood head and dusty shoulders above its fellow-captives.

It did not matter which way I turned, there was the army of the dead. I wondered if all of them were now extinct. Did it make any real difference, if they were? There are still birds, and sea mammals and reptiles and amphibians and invertebrates. In any event it can be argued, I said to myself, that there are still auks in the world, and dodos, and golden toads, black-faced honeycreepers, pupfish, wrasses, tree snails. There are the preserved specimens. Here before me, in this cold room, so cold my bones are breaking, here I can see that many of the properties of such things are extant still, their form and colour, for example, the length of their flight-feathers, and the morphology of their feet. But not the way they walk, or their peculiarities of mating ritual. That's gone. The mechanics through which their evolution was linked with their prey or an original whose deadly marks they mimicked. That's gone, too.

By the time my phone-alarm rang at six I was still wading through instances and bewildered by them, everything I looked at seemed to have an avalanche of knock-on effects, every bird and every butterfly in its setting, and my mind was running about amidst Escher staircases, lemniscates, Moebius strips, and an infinity of microscopic life pullulating in the impression left by a passing hoof, and finally relief came. I found a framework with which to make a sort of sense of the blizzard of consequences. I recalled a fable from school. The fox, who knew many things, and the hedgehog, who knew one big thing. I was surrounded with the relics of hedgehogs who all had known one answer to one big question: how to survive in the environment they had inherited. Taxidermy had preserved some of their properties, and death had donated one of its own—silence. It was the hedgehog property in each of the multitude of variations that became extinct and irrecoverable.

I fell instantly asleep.

A couple of hours' dreamless snoring set me up. I felt smug about being prepared for any situation, with basic food and water. I was confident that uncontactable Fann would find a way to get me to fresh air soon. He would worry, surely he would worry when he did not hear from me this morning. He always knew someone to bribe, and Christenson House did not pay its security guards well. I concentrated on making sure we were ready to run with our haul when the chance came.

I eked out my supplies, and also my occupation, stringing out for the whole day my exploration of foreign lands through their relicts. My main delaying tactic was to start my own list. I went shelf by shelf, detailing everything I thought we could flog to a collector. My guts tingled at these treasures, I whispered exclamations, made plans. No one except me knows. Fann had dealt with me fairly in the past, he would be in clover. I could hear him now, corks popping and phone buzzing discreetly. My room bloomed—I would buy direct from artists, not through galleries. I knew a shop in Den Haag that sold Persian rugs. I could have *stained glass* in the conservatory. I would never need to leave. I could sit in silence, undisturbed, and at peace.

At the same time, as the day spooled out slowly, there was an accumulated uneasiness. To begin with, what Fann called 'a little storage bay' was massive. I thought 'cubby-hole' when I walked in first, but I plundered details from row after row and shelf after shelf, packed with variations on the theme of extinction. There was a Chinese River Dolphin overhead, a rhino-sized turtle, a stuffed snake. There was a twelve-foot moa, neck stretched like an angry gander. I made my rounds of the room, concentrating on details, unstacking and re-stacking boxes and cases twice and three times over.

Periodically, I returned to the door with its smooth, cool panels, but never a handle could I find. It was very warm, too.

And not quite as silent as I would like.

Fann in his cups once excoriated the human impulse for collecting specimens—can't just leave a thing to be, he spat, mere arrogance making us act, we have to comment, make everything have a role that explains something about us. It was no more *scientific investigation* than picking flowers to decorate a buttonhole. So, what I am doing is picking flowers and admittedly, it is not well-thought of, that one should take flowers from a grave. On the other hand, unlike Howard Carter and his lauded tribe, I'm not robbing an actual grave.

Silence is a property of death.

The second evening fell, and I returned to the blanket, and the straw and to wakeful, uneasy occupation of a bed that felt more and more like a display case. It could not literally be true that all the specimens were facing me. I left only one light on, so that I could see fewer eyes. Of the assembled items I was contracted to take, the auk was the tallest on the table. White patches gleamed and its glass eye glittered, even under its dust. Its label had told me how the birds were pursued, one strangled and one held prisoner on a boat for three days before being stoned to death as a witch.

Such an intimate way to commit murder, strangulation. The auk was about the size of a toddler, so this was no quick seize-and-snap, though being built for the ocean dive, the pursuit over land could only end one way. But once seized, the snap must have been harder won. Even immobilized the bird must have struggled—hard to imagine, looking at the auk now: stationary and with the harmless, defenceless air of the eternal victim. Who knows what it might have been like in life?

I woke in the middle of the night, cast adrift from memory. I had been dreaming—I was trapped somewhere in the dark, my feet were tied. All I could hear was the sound of pounding, stones grinding, the shell, the fragile shell, smashing and the crunching boot smearing the chick over the bare rock.

The early English and the Norse called it a razorbill, a spear-bird—is that what provoked that most personal of killing? The hooked beak dowsing for blood, and the hurt, enraged sailor pinioning the tiny wings? The neck seized as firmly as an untethered sail? Anger driving the throttling fingers as hard as cold rocks and the palpitating heart battering and shuddering in its downy velvet? The other auk trussed by the feet, in a boat for three days, starving, before the stoning started and meaningless death advanced.

The odd thing about this place is that each time I ventured through, there were parts I seemed to have missed. I hunted around the shelves again in the illogical but electrifying hope that I would find the handle on the door—or another door— and that I could escape somewhere, Atlantis, Narnia, Xanadu, anywhere. In searching I found only more display cases, including a small one on a trolley. The glass was broken and it was empty. The glass was broken from the inside.

Evening fell again. I had very little water left, and very little food.

Silence is…

Silence is one of the ways in which these animals are extinct, now that I think of it. This thought was company, it had the reassurance of a bromide. Sound as well as presence removed from the world. The particular scuttle of an animal, their particular voice. The snuffling of dim-sighted animals who specialized in snouts.

My nerves were on their last legs because apart from every- thing else, I was waiting for the generator to run down. It shouldn't, it was not supposed to, but I knew that it would.

I remembered my dream, the chase, the crackling shell, and the crunching of the half-formed chick. The moment not only of death but of extinction. That's another thing about humans. The death of a human is a tragedy, the extinction of another species is survival of the fittest. I tried to visualize half a billion dead in an Australian wildfire. It was like trying to imagine the experience of eternity. Also, any cooked animal, even an imag- inary one, looked like food to me by now, so the experiment made me feel extremely hungry, but rather guilty.

The generator began a droning purr. I knew it. It was ready to run down now, I knew it. Of course. I had a pencil-sized torch ready in my hand. But when the dark did come, when it seized me, I dropped the torch and the length of time it took to hit the floor and clatter was enough time, enough silence, for me to let fall the sound of shock. My heart was pulsating like a trapped bird. Darkness had joined the silence.

From some sunken fold of my fear-shrunken brain there leaked this—not fact so much as resonance—from my dewy youth when I had confidence in my grasp on things. Einstein said that God did not play dice, despite having fairly much proved that He did, but Boltzmann before him had promulgated a hard-bitten gambler of a deity. It is improbable, says the bold Boltzmann, that all the particles of warm air in a room will gather in one corner, improbable that an ordered universe exists. But it is not, mathematically, impossible. There could be a fluctuation from disorder to order.

And I would have been less shocked at the fleeting appearance of a disembodied brain, or terrified by the realization that I was the only self-aware being in existence, than I was at what actually happened in the dark.

In that cubicle of a place as measureless, dark, and silent as a well, there was a sound, a boom, the harsh cry a raven might make, when you don't know if it is aggression or amour. But that was just the keynote. A tuning-fork. There was no mistaking what follows: a choir of lost voices.

They had the whole range. From basso profundo to trills so high they were not so much a sound as a shimmer, a sparkle in the unforgiving darkness. It was dark as pitch, no sound or shape to act as a pole star whence I might determine my longitude among these dead. The mournful honking like a foghorn might have been the moa. Something sounded like a stoned woodpecker. A wooden sphere rattling down through a hollow branch. Purrings. Clucking. It was an April of birdsong, sweet showers of duets, drenching coloratura warbles, clicks and hoots and honks and bittern-booms tunnelling like roots beneath. Then all the small chirruping fowl ceased their melody, falling instantly silent at the bereft, angry shriek of a raptor.

The noise rolled on, and I listened and tried to rise above it, deny it. Curated wildlife is not expected to hold any secrets. They have been measured and tagged. Look at them, they've got a label. Not autonomy, but a lovely label. There must be an explanation.

No explanation revealed itself, but finally there was the transformative moment when what was happening, being beyond denial or subjugation, became meaningful. The Copernican Principle—that we are not privileged observers—applies to planets and galaxies and auks and Zanzibar leopards and thieves. If the auk is here, why not me? There will still be humans, even if I don't get out of this room. Technology can reproduce the sounds a dead thing made by looking at the way its voice-box was constructed. We will be able to reproduce the sounds of the nightingale or the whale, when they have been finally extinguished. Scientists could reproduce my voice-box, but not the words that came babbling out unheard, of my room, of heritage-series paints, and her hair like corn-silk, reclaimed wood for the floors, and polished granite.

It was not a comforting moment. Those that are truly transformative never are. But it felt peculiarly opportune. The moment on the first night, whenever that was, two days ago, a year, the moment that I realized I would not finish the job in the hours I had allotted. That moment just now, two hours ago, of greeting extinction—both disconcerting but both bringing peacefulness. Resolution.

The ancient Greeks drew a distinction between quantitative time and qualitative time, the right, the opportune time. How long have I been here, have I been here long enough? I have Chronos and Kairos enough for such thoughts now. I literally know neither the day nor the hour, and the noise goes on and more voices join in, and they meld together into a soundscape so crowded that no perspective can be found. I have the space in which I lie and nothing more, not courage, not hope. It is the twilight of those who have thought they were gods, and the hammer will fall where it will, without regard to the innocence or complicity of those beneath.

More than anything it is borne in upon me, with a conviction I have not known since childhood, that I am of no consequence. I am already smashed to atoms. Nothing left but bones and a jerry-can of piss, nameless as a coursed hare or a baited bear.

Silence is a property of death.

Hell Hath No Fury

THE EYELIDS were definitely not going to open this morning. Every other morning it had been a struggle, but this morning, it was not going to happen. A moment of panic, then, when she realized that they were not just heavy, they were actually gummed together. Maybe this was the next thing, she thought, fighting down the flush of fear, perhaps this was the next stage. She sat up in bed. No. It would be alright. A gentle rub, moistening her finger, and they opened. She could see. Her mouth was so dry it hurt, down to the back of her throat and the root of her tongue was so parched it was almost cracked. Her eyes were still heavy, and ached deeply. She had always hated hangovers. She particularly hated having them when she hadn't been drinking.

There was a mirror on the wall opposite her bed. Her name had been stencilled across the top on large blue letters. When she sat up in the bed, the first thing she saw was her own face with 'LIBBY' captioned across it. She had been here for three years, if one could still measure time, and her looks had not changed at all. Her hair was long, straight and brown, her eyes small and blue. She looked impassively at her reflection and it smiled back at her. There was a definite gloat in the smile. Libby didn't like that. She swung her legs out of bed, and stood up, organizing in her mind what she had to do today.

The kitchen was filthy, though she had tidied it the night before. A bulging, stinking bag of rubbish slumped in the corner and the sink was piled with dishes, encrusted pans poking at angles out of the basin, pools of water on the floor, smudges on the window. She felt the usual plummet of despair and she fought against it. The neighbours turned on their radio and the music shook her windows, pummelled her aching ears. Libby balanced on one leg as she filled the kettle with water, resting her elbow against the low metal sink and letting her mind wander. There were always memories. They waited for her, in the shadows of her mind, they waited patiently for her to find them. She could see one. There was sunshine in it, creeping around the corner of some dark, cool house, a dress, there was something … Even as her eyelids drooped, Libby saw the slug twist is head up out of the spout of the kettle. A filthy picture of boiled slug was crushed down; she removed the lid and carefully carried the slug out into the back yard. The yard was filled with concrete and had been spotless the night before. Now, despite the high stone walls, the concrete was newly patterned with catshit and vomit.

Libby shut the door. She made coffee but the milk had gone off and there was no food. She refused to be defeated, she determined that, today, she would manage to get something to eat when she went downtown to do her shopping. Hastily swallowing the bitter brew, she gathered her purse and her shopping list together and left the house, without looking into any of the mirrors which were dusted about the house. She knew, from long experience, that the freshly laundered clothes she had put on that morning would already be stained and crumpled. If she looked at them, she would become embarrassed and self-conscious and there was nothing she could do about them.

She walked into town, looking neither left nor right. People jostled her, children smeared their sticky fingers on her, harried shoppers dug the sharp corners of their purchases into her legs. She kept one thought in her mind. There were only two things she had to do today. She had to go to the bank and lodge some money, and then she had to go to the supermarket. In the supermarket she had to buy five things. One bottle of milk. One loaf of bread. One bag of carrots. One piece of fish. One bag of apples. If she concentrated really hard, perhaps nothing would slip away from her. Perhaps she would get there and back as logic might decree.

The sun was in her eyes all the way into town. She did not have any sunglasses and she discovered, to her annoyance, that she was now wearing a heavy woollen overcoat. She crossed the street to walk in the shade but, miraculously, the directions all changed and the sun shone relentlessly, making her squint. She could feel her face flushing, she started to sweat and to feel grubby. By the time she got to the bank, she was sure that people standing beside her could smell her, and indeed, the whole queue turned to stare at her as she came in. As quickly as she could she slipped off her heavy coat, and with a carefree toss of her head, she took her place in the queue. Everyone around her was scrubbed and fresh and smooth, she looked jealously at their clothes. Her wrists were itchy and she knew without looking down what had happened —her clothes had shrunk again. Her ill-fitting trousers now flapped above her ankles, her sweater, now thick blue wool, stopped short everywhere.

The queue moved up a notch or two and a few more customers joined onto the end. Libby moved uncomfortably from foot to foot. Her back hurt and she was starting to get stomach cramps. With a sudden horrified recognition, she realized that her period was starting, again, there and then. She forced the feeling down. All it meant was six things to buy in the supermarket. People were staring at her. She tilted her head up and pretended she didn't notice, but couldn't hide the ugly red flush that was spreading from her neck to her face. Her scalp prickled.

The queue moved quickly along, so quickly that Libby began to let herself hope that perhaps this particular trial would not happen that day. Customer after customer made their way to the little booth, exchanged a few words with the teller, a few chimes of merry laughter blossomed, the customer, with crisp rustles of silk and linen, strode away. The woman in front of Libby moved forward. She was rummaging in her bag. She glanced behind her. Libby looked up. There was a pale sheen, like a shield, over the dark irises of the woman's eyes. She smiled faintly as she wrenched from some inner pocket a huge sheaf of papers. Libby fought down the burning impulse to burst into tears. Instead she sighed deeply, resigned herself to the situation, forcing her thoughts to be calm, to be unaffected, to be cheerful in her resignation. But in private, if that delicate treasure existed anymore, she vowed fiercely never to be fooled again.

Three quarters of an hour later, the woman, the unwitting instrument of Libby's torture, was finished. She turned away from the booth. The sheen was gone from her eyes, she looked confused and upset. Her bag was now impossibly swollen beyond its capacity, and, struggling with the weight, she lifted her arm and looked at her watch. Libby bit her lip. The woman's face flooded with disbelief and anguish. Then she, too, bit her lip and tilted her chin up. She tried to smooth down her clothes, but, as her thin hand passed over her stomach, a thin squeak of protest escaped. The woman was five months pregnant. She clenched her teeth, her eyes filled with tears, and she marched out of the bank. Libby reluctantly shuffled forward, and did not dare look back.

The moment she reached the booth, the moment her hand touched to smooth and varnished wood, she knew she was lost. The teller couldn't hear her at first, and impatiently shook her head and inclined her ear to the glass. Libby was yelling with all her might but whispered mumbles were all that emerged. Her breath, to which the teller reacted with distaste, misted the glass. Though she had had only two things to do when she came in, they had maliciously multiplied and she, too, was taking sheaf after sheaf of paper from her pockets. Her brain was heavy and dull, her words came out in staggered confusion and warm, noisy air filled her ears. For every transaction the teller had to get a superior or an assistant, everything had to be rearranged and adapted. When she escaped, Libby looked at her watch. She had been there almost an hour.

The breeze was blessedly cool on her face when she stepped out of the bank and it gave her a momentary courage. Dammit, she would make a run for the park. There had to be advent-ages, Libby thought, hoisting her now multiplied bags onto her shoulder, to persistent lying and pretence. When you wanted to do it for yourself, you had had a lot of practice.

There was the big main park, where ice-creams fell to the ground and children were stung by wasps, and Libby was careful to walk with measured paces through the curlicued wrought iron gates, with her usual expression of calm acceptance nailed to her face. If there was even a hint of anything else, she might be caught. If the merest trace of any other feeling—anger, resentment, defiance—was spotted in her face, she might give everything away. The park was bright and the pond stinking and cats stole surreptitiously through the hedges. Libby pretended not to see them. She made her way down the concrete path, smiling slightly when she tripped on the protruding roots of trees that had shattered the concrete. The small park was nearby, she could feel it. She blanked every thought from her mind and stepped forward again and again.

Today would be a rare day.

The little park was quiet and plain and full of emotions. There were some other people there, already and they glanced up at her when she stepped from a tree. No one spoke but they smiled at her, a co-conspirator. Libby's feet made the slightest noise, subtle as a Vermeer light, on the moist peat. She sat on the glossy wooden bench.

Beech leaves dappled the sunlight onto the dark earth and clumps of bright flowers dotted thick tree trunks and lurked near patches of fern. The air was heavy and quiet. There was a choice of faint noises to hear, depending on the wishes of the listener. Distant music, chattering voices, rain, waves on a beach. The park, that brief universe, was full of animals. A lion made its heavy way past, a snake looped round a branch, a wolf curled up to sleep, hens pecked in the grass, snails copulated on leaves, a ladybird poised on a trembling blade of grass. Far away to the east of the Castle, the tinkle and giggle of the waterfall. The Castle wasn't always a castle, though some saw old-fashioned turrets and leaded windows, or a squat reminder of a vague Middle Age. Others saw a wonder of modernistic glass, or a cool wooded farmhouse, a Palladian mansion or even a plain white cottage. Libby didn't look. She didn't want to make decisions, she wanted only to appreciate the unexpected gift. A woman sat down beside her and took Libby's hand into her own smooth dry palm.

How could she ever have thought it made sense? The park was the only place for all these years where Libby could bear to think about what had brought her here. Every other minute of her life was squeezed out in trying to struggle against the unavoidable distresses and humiliations that were her days. Here she could endure taking out the tightly wrapped memories and feel the regret, feel the dismay in her veins. It had made sense at the time. Her parents were querulous and congenitally unhappy. They fought and bickered at every opportunity and had nothing but discontent to keep them company in the wait for the end.

Year after year of planning her escape. She had written the script of her departure from their thinning lives and promised herself—nothing much. That was true. Nothing more than somewhere quiet and small and her own. She wanted a small neat flat where she did not have exasperated glances thrown her if she put the radio on at more than a whisper. She had worked out her finances, and knew that she could afford to have the heating on when it was cold and not have tight remarks made about waste and indulgence and have fingerless gloves left pointedly on her bed. All her energy was spent knowing that she could never get it right but feeling obsessively obliged to keep trying. Rather like here, Libby thought. She had become addicted to the belief that perseverance would succeed.

So she had never left. She dressed to suit the squabbling duo who claimed her life, she bought them endless treats that were never quite right, drove them wherever their whim took them. The belief that she wanted only to keep her parents happy was her only belief. A deity, an afterlife, these had not been rejected but simply dropped by the wayside, a mislaid book or a bag dropped from a car. When the end came, when she had put her nurtured idea into practice, she had truly convinced herself that she was doing it for the sake of her mother and father. If she couldn't leave them—confident of the car's airbag, she jammed her foot on the accelerator and headed for the tree—then they would leave her. It would be quick and painless and a sadness which would lessen.

Libby remembered being a small child, being introverted and over-thoughtful. Libby is herself, her mother would say, with only slight spite. She meant that Libby's view of things always was a little off centre, always a little strange. Even Libby had known not to tell her mother that her younger daughter was quite excited at the prospect of death. Libby had been twelve when she had realized that this inevitable horizon was exciting. When she died, she thought, she would know the secrets of the world. The questions, which had puzzled philosophers and scientists and theologians, would be known by an anonymous, insignificant girl. When it came it was not at all what she had expected.

There was Cerberus, but not as the drawings had shown. There was the river Styx, the grey and hollow-cheeked dead of the Greeks, the vividness of the medieval imagination, fire, cloven hoof, appalling distortions of the human form, hideous punishment. But these things were at a different level to Libby, as people who live in countries of extreme situations can often lead quite unremarkable lives. The screams and the stench went on but they did not come down her street because she had never feared them in life. Instead, tailor-made to reflect the diminutive terrors that had made up her diminutive life, Libby was not punished with the unspeakable but with the unbearable.

The woman turned Libby's hand over, palm up, and smiled at her once more. Libby smiled back and was filled with a magnificent, bone shaking gratitude. The park was an accident, unobserved, unspoken, valued like a fragile precious life, a glimpse of what she could have had had she not, in blindness and stubbornness, thrown her life away years before she had set foot in a car. She followed the woman into the sunlight and into the woman's own version of the park, a winter wood with snow-bowed trees and a stone house with a fire and a deep, silken rug. The woman's skin was at once warm and cool, her touch firm, her eyes sad and bright. I don't care, Libby thought, recklessness rushing up through her, it is worth whatever happens.

When she woke up, Libby was lying on a hot parched pavement. She raised her head just as a woman stepped over her, and the woman's heel caught Libby over the back of her head. The woman made a disgusted little noise and hurried on. A second later, the stink of vomit reached Libby's nostrils and coinstantaneously she felt the acrid residue in her mouth, the last undigested lumps in her throat. Out of habit she smiled, like she didn't mind anything, and struggled to her feet. Her hair was filthy and stood on end. Her nails were broken and jagged, dirt seamed her hands. Arrayed around her was her shopping, now magically multiplied to fourteen or fifteen bags. One was split and a two-litre bottle of some sweet soft drink poked out. Never mind, she said, there are buses and taxis. Libby regained her balance and looked around. After the coldness of the woman's park, the heat seemed suddenly tropical, Libby's scalp prickled with sweat and her face reddened. She was wearing stiletto white shoes which were a size too big for her, she could hardly walk on them.

She staggered over to her bags, feeling ill and hot and sore. The shirt she wore had once been white—Oh Christ she said aloud. My uniform. Her school uniform, her hated uniform, her hated school. A white shirt that impassively recalled the fretted mornings she spent in painful anxiety that there would be something wrong, something she would only realize under the disdainful scrutiny of her dark-eyed rich companions. (We sacrificed to send you to a good school, her mother had reminded her endlessly. For what? You thought my inferiority complex was not developed?) Now the shirt was streaked with grey and had a dribble of egg-yolk down the shiny red tie. Maybe they won't notice, Libby thought firmly. She could feel that the cloth under her arms was damp, dark with sweat. She had no skirt. Well, no skirt, no memory and the paralysing conviction that the zip was gaping as you approached the blackboard.

She looked down at her legs. They were stocky now, like they belonged to someone else, someone burly. But they looked fragile, too, corrugated with a mountain range of varicose veins that had a tender look to them, like the slightest knock would rupture them. Her skin was strangely bubbled, blistered like a cabbage-leaf. Libby, never vain, almost wept. She promised herself that, once home, she would—she *would* —recall the details of her beautiful afternoon. Libby gathered her bags and struggled off, the thin plastic handles of the bags cutting into her hands. A few individuals and then a small group of people passed her and she glanced into their faces, seeing the familiar repugnance reflected in their expressions. One, after he had passed her, turned and threw some coins in her direction. The path to her house receding inch by inch into the blazing grey distance.

The Last March of the King of Laois

THERE WERE cattle lowing, distant but loud, big bass single notes. Crows were calling in short, harsh bursts; singly the sounds were without variance or modulation, but the call-and-response seemed to pick out some formal geometry. A magpie chattered out its rattling notes, and far away, up on the twisted and undulating road through the bog, a succession of car doors answered. Grass outlined broken tracks of peat between the clumps of brassy furze and the scattered groves of hazel and birch. The trees were stunted, and in stunning colours: twigs red and glossy as jam, bark as white as milk, and their leaves as bright as sequins. The sky overhead was story-book blue, with cirrus clouds. The hills were piebald in navy and slate, and a bank of chunky grey cumulus rested on the horizon.

> "It was said that from the mid-point of the middle hill, a person could see the conjunction of the four ancient kingdoms, the single point where they touched each other; this meeting of royal boundaries happened on a bog, a boundary between worlds."

The workers clustered together, and the breeze whipped words into rags. They stood at a crossing-point, where the crooked path crossed a die-straight drain filled with water that looked almost décolleté under a thin skin of algae. They were piecing out the day's work. There had been talk, at the beginning of the job, of inoculating the bog with sphagnum moss from an adjoining one, that was untouched and flourishing since being re-wetted two years ago. Two or three of the conservationists had been to that other bog earlier, just a visit, just to the edges of a small lake that glimmered blackly, its edges thick with reeds and rushes. They had stood like penitents hovering at the church door, doubtful of welcome. The ground had been supple but tough there, like the flank of a cow. Where they stood now was soft, but working the bog had dried it out, there was no spring in it anymore. The debate had gone round for a couple of days, but yesterday, they decided not to disturb what had been repaired, decided to leave well enough alone. A few voices tried now to resurrect discussion, but were curtly over-ruled. *There's every reason to believe that this will be enough.* A few more words, lost on a gust of cold air. Kit bags were lifted to demonstrate preparedness, directions given as though thrown from the palm. The group disbanded. Very faintly, from high above them, came the disconcertingly frail peeping of a buzzard.

Three people walked down to the borrow-pit. There had been debate about this, also, about whether this pit had yielded enough peat already, if maybe it should be left in peace. But the conservationists had decided that since so little extra was required now to finish blocking the drain, the borrow-pit could lend more without coming to harm. The three volunteers carried containers, and trowels, and decided amongst themselves how to divide up the remaining work, and how to stagger their breaks. They were relieved to get to work. The sun was blazing, but it was too early in the year for any real heat in it. The wind was very cold, too. The corvids were wheeling and calling, and the yelling—comparative to its size—of a wren was ruffled around with the lace of small birds' songs. There was the brackish smell from the water, and the scent of coconuts from the fiery gorse (the volunteers had a mock argument: gorse, furze, or whin?) They settled down to the work, found the best positions, noticed or ignored the constant sounds of slight movements, and the flashes of a million pinhead suns on wing-cases. Previous fuel-cutting from the peatland had opened an even earlier working, a small rectangle, sunken to a depth of a few thousand years.

"It was a theory that bog bodies were deposited along tribal boundaries in Iron Age kingship rituals. Ritually killed, ritually marked, they turned to leather under the heather, they and the bog together, rattle-bags of beliefs."

The volunteers worked on, eventually in silence. One of the trowels broke so when the bell rang for first tea-break, two people walked back to the tent. One remained. She got up to stretch her legs, with the usual clicks and cracks of encroaching middle age, and walked up and down, walking to the sunken working, stretching, walking down and up. Some peat, stacked on the side of the sunken space, had fallen away. Bending to look at the layers was more callisthenics than curiosity.

The skin of the corpse was rippled like wet sand. When the body had been buried, or flung, its head had twisted round to its shoulder, and was facing out, towards the hills. The eyes had rotted away, leaving tight little circles of layered leather, like an abandoned shell. The nose was crushed out of sight. This crushing had pulled the cheek and mouth to one side, making a faintly sheepish expression, as though something they feared might be unwelcome must be said. From under the black, kneaded layer of peat, the embedded links of a backbone had been exposed, and a twist of something very red, as ruby, or Mars, protruded.

The sun was very hot, the sky bright, the wind slicing. Around about her were hillocks of lime-green grass, and rusted crowns of reeds, scattered so unsystematically that the black earth looked balding, a vegetative alopecia. The surrounding stretch of bog was striped like plaid, in truffle and biscuit colours, and dotted here and there by ashy shrubs, dangling their fiery baubles of dead fruit. The third volunteer lay down on her front and wriggled closer. She peered disbelievingly at what had been unveiled. Stretching out her hand as though to a wild animal, she eventually touched the twist of red. It might have been the root of some plant upon which the corpse had died. Conceivably it was hair. Absent-mindedly she picked away at some more peat.

> dried face of what might have been a king
> consequences   sacrifices   atonement   appeasement
> throats got cut, necks got wrung, or sharp blades
> turned the insides outside, and bodies pinned to
> the pit or pool with withies
> buried in their leather, mostly, some with
> a cap or a belt, or an artisan garrotte

She turned her mind from the jumble of remembered details. She wondered what was best to do. They would need to tell a museum about it, about

> animals were sacrificed too—dismembered
> horses, hounds, pups   that film, the great burning,
> eyeless figure, the happy hieratic killers, singing *Sumer
> is Icumen In*   not always a question of sacrifice
> they disfigured kings, disputed or overturned kings, to
> make them unfit
> either way, believing it was necessary, though. Death

She lay on the ground by the edge of the borrow-pit, and looked across the bog from the corpse's perspective. She felt sheltered. A shrub of some sort stood directly between her and the sun, chopping up the sunlight before it fell on her. It was too dense a silhouette to be identified, and its thin, whippy branches sprang and trailed like escaping harp-strings. Past her feet was a hummock of reeds, dark-hearted, and an illumin-ated nimbus, like a caterpillar, curled against the light.

Bogs were carbon sinks, that was why she was here, trusting that she had been told the truth. Helpless to do anything else in the face of the enormity of destruction and devastation of the planet on which she stood, she did as she was told in the way she was told to do it, and trusted that the bog, if revital-ized, would take it from there.

Forests covered everything, thousands of years ago, except for bogs. If a tree falls and no-one hears it, did it fall? They would need to tell a museum about what had come to light, this corpse. The re-wetting of the bog would have to stop.

Turning over in her grave, the low bank of peat was topped with a dense, black line of contorted branches, spattered with a spray of buttery crumbs of flowers. The grass on the side of the bank looked wiry, but also as though the black and olive and bleached, milky strands were woven. Turning again, onto her other side, turned to face the corpse, she regarded the wrinkled pouches that had been its eyes. She inched her face as close to his as she could without touching it, so his face loomed like a close-up photograph. She had a weakness for documentaries about the dead, bog-bodies and mummies, dried-out inhabitants of caves. In some sensitized part of her mind, as a reflex, a Pavlovian synaesthesia, she could hear the sort of plummy voice that always seemed to do the voice-overs.

"The contents of the stomach would reveal that the death had occurred in the early part of the year, in what would now be March. The last meal, eaten about twelve hours before death, was a gruel made of fifty-seven different types of seeds, including yarrow, barley, fat hen, buttercup, nettles, goosefoot, and flax. Fifty years ago, two archaeologists made up a porridge, a gruel, based on the contents of a bog body dug out in Denmark. They concluded that your man was better off in the bog than facing this muck for his breakfast. But the point had been that the sacrifice carried in his bag—his belly, if you prefer—as gifts to the altar, the seeds of those plants which were depended upon for survival. Seeds as emblem of survival and the means to it, emblem of generation and the means to it."

Most of the body was under the peat. The backbone curved into the light, the upper arm, the shoulder, and the face still flaked with peat. Embedded into the flesh of the arm were some protrusions, firm to the tip of her finger where she tentatively touched them. They could have been anything, some meaningless twig, but she wondered if those who had killed him had pinioned him into his grave, dead or alive. To be on the safe side.

"Breaks in the bones, or apparent scalping, is often the result of the weight of the peat, and not of pre-mortem violence. However, in the case of this find, there were traces of deliberate injury, in the form of lacerations to the breast. A wound of this sort suggests that the victim was a king, or was attempting to be so crowned. A king had to be free of physical imperfections. That was a law that applied to even a god like Nuada Airgetlám, so could not be dodged by a mere human attempting to act as an intermediary between the known world, the physical world, the world of rain, and broken fingers, and intestinal parasites, and the world of concrete abstracts. A king negotiated powers that were less tangible than miot or the phosphorescence of decay, but that extracted revenge if not propitiated, and an imperfection, however slight, was not a risk worth running. This contender had had his nipples cut off, their absence symbolic of the king's inability to feed and nurture his people, his land, his *tuath*, both land, and people. Politicians might reconsider public life if reneging on election promises demanded body-parts, or a life."

The body was the same colour as the trees, the burnt-earth branches that were speckled with tan and ruby and apple-green leaves. The crows were still singing but the smaller birds had been hushed by the dark silhouette of the buzzard, coasting the cold gusts while he hunted the chiaroscuro sky. She wondered what unnamed colours the bird saw when it turned its disapproving yellow eye to her. Looking towards the lapis lazuli horizon from where she lay on the ground, the bog looked felted and downy. The scudding clouds were small but grey as basalt, occulting the sun and draining away all the colour from the earth, then sped on, letting the sun blaze and saturate the land, turning the burial-tanned skin to the colour of gleaming chestnuts. She huddled like a leveret against the bare ground.

      this death is become a work of art, being open
to interpretation   If a king loses the contest,
  someone is sent violently to appease the gods of the
  harvests, and the sacrifice is no longer understood,
  does it still have meaning?

They would have to tell someone, a museum

    vanity, too - a trace of beard under his chin.
    Had he missed it shaving, on the last day of his
life? Or was it all that was left of a beard?
                 Fragile   approaching
  the bog, on the last day of his life or dead already
  and brought to the bog, a carried corpse? Or striding
  to a conflict? Or collared as the sacrifice and stoned
  off his nipple-free tits maybe if he knew what waited
      those burned as witches sometimes were
  given hallucinogens, ergot, something to kill the pain
  but earlier, here, there was no myth of genesis, nor
  afterlife. You came out from the dark, you went back to
  the dark

or hovered, eternally on duty, in the borderlands
            borderlands require, demand, their guardians

when the throttled man was taken from Tollund Fen in
Denmark, one of the workers died. Cardiac arrest. It is said
that if a body is taken from the bog,

                    rivers, too, trees, even bridges

that if a body is taken from the bog, the bog will take another.
    They would have to call a museum, tell them about the
body. She sat up, and looked about her. The specialists were
too far away to summon. They looked like standing stones, at
this distance. One was upright, holding a rod, one was bent,
resting its hands on its knees. The wind brought occasional
tatters of voices from the tea-tent. People were always finding
stuff in bogs. The peat cut away

    irreplaceable peat cut away to heat replaceable people
                                        a bit bitter
        photographs of winter-wrapped people like shawled
        igloos   that distrustful stare at the camera
                uncles describing throwing the sods up and
        grandfathers' pernickety rules about tidiness in stooking
        footing stacking   manuscripts   the accidentally dead
        combs, animals, shrines, coins, relics of war

"There were no defensive cuts on this body, unlike, for
example, Old Croghan Man. A full excavation would
have revealed this body to be naked except for a short
cloak made of calf-skin, a plaited leather belt, and a
leather band around one calf. Exceptionally, it would
be discovered that the cloak contained a pouch,
possibly a pocket, in which were stored some pieces of
flint, some seeds, and an object of unclear function,

made of horn. No amount of excavation would have revealed the remainder of the clothing, as linen did not survive the acidic environment. The throat had been cut almost to the bone, there was a deep gash in the chest over the heart, and a hole smashed in the back of the head. Any one of the injuries would have caused death. The multiplicity of fatal injuries betokens, not an excessive rage or a form of torture, but an economic attitude. A deity could hold multiple portfolios: fertility, a generous earth, war, death, sovereignty. Multiple means of murder meant multiple simultaneous offerings to a deity in all its forms. Streamlining sacrifice, as you might say."

Once announced, the discovery would take on a life of its own. The re-wetting would have to stop, standing back for the archaeologists, and the curators, and the historians, and the journalists. The body would take the name of the bog, become its defining feature. The bog would be important because of the body it had preserved.

the people and the land, land and people, a
price paid for protection, for prosperity, not posterity.
the fact of miraculous preservation,
not the significance of the leather and bones
preserved

"The probability that the man, when alive, did little manual labour would have been suggested by the mani-cured nails, and undamaged hands. His age would have been reckoned at between forty and fifty. The figure was tall for the time, about 5'10", and had all his teeth, though two molars would have shown signs of decay which would, eventually, if he hadn't been chopped about to honour a deity, have caused him great pain.

So, everything is relative, really—anyone in the grip of unrelievable toothache might well welcome the whack of a priest's axe to the back of the head."

       propitiatory sacrifice, a material offering for protection against the abstracts   hunger, failure, annihilation, the fearful unknowable   the appointed, maybe anointed, one, dispatched and laid in the ground

          and the ground carefully chosen, too, sanctified by its own form   now bogs are *mamba*, miles and miles of bugger-all but then,
    then bogs were open fearlessly to the heavens, when forests shrouded, sheltered, everything else bogs mixed worlds, water and earth, death and a form of not-death, suspended death

         protection against the abstracts
    protection for the material world from the immaterial, vital immaterial not *immaterial* immaterial
  for all the material world and all that lived materially in it the lung-like bog, the peat sinking quantities of carbon   all the boiling life under the surface of the earth the constant dynamic, the exudates of roots signalling and receiving, the rhizosphere as alive as a brain with electrochemical messaging
         all the boiling life on the surface
  let the dead lie where they fall
       let the life teem beneath them
  let the dead lie where they fall

She picked her trowel up from where she had left it among the anonymous asphodels. She began piling wet peat over the body, covering it, returning its grave to it.

She could not say exactly where the face had come into the light and she felt a brief, violent panic, as though an abyss had been revealed, as though her decision had brought with it some catastrophic consequence. The feeling passed. She waited by the graveside.

> "Had the excavation been completed, it would have been revealed that a number of objects had been buried with the sacrificial victim, the *christos*. Some vessels containing food, a bowl of butter, and a short spear. A large hound would have been found, slaughtered and buried with its head under the corpse's hand. A surprising amount of the human's soft tissue was preserved, including the brain, stomach, heart, and the liver. The trachea and vocal cords had survived also, would have been subject to three-dimensional printed replication, and, via the prosthesis of electronic signals, would have yielded the sound of the sacrifice's voice."

There was a hiss, like a brushed cymbal, that seemed to be the noise of a hot day. Crickets were clicking like metronomes. A bee was working in the gorse, flower to flower, four beats to the bar, ninety beats to the minute; a patch of heather thick with bees, buzzing like a harpsichord. Tiny birds rocked on the branch-tops, fiddlers bowing the branches across the raw air. The cattle, still happily distant, were off again with their close-harmony *basso profundo*. The buzzard flew overhead again, still hunting, wheeling away and towards the veiled hills.

Each Tether Has Its End

THE THICKNESS of the air makes the bells ring out. It's not the time of year for them, but not a blade of corn between the hounds of the Hunter, so, church-bells. Church-bells ringing like mad things, then alarms, sirens, warning systems in hospitals, mortuaries, dam-walls. The wind changes with those who pass overhead. The bells, the mechanical shrieks of the cities, are dragged in our wake, our echoing soundtrack, their reverberations will knock planes from the sky. The stormy petrel will ride the soundwaves.

Parker said querulously,

"It isn't the time of year for bells. I mean, WTAF? Too early for sleighbells and Christmas chimes and that shit."

Appearing to shut his eyes, he squinted at Hardy. The security lamps cut Hardy's face in two, one side queasy in a grubby primrose light, the other in greenish shadow. Parker thought about Hardy's face being beautiful and almond-shaped, but the realization that his own was more a walnut configuration made him pettish. He said,

"Or maybe I'm wrong."

He attempted to inject a little piteousness into his voice. It came out too strongly, and Hardy thought Parker was joking, and laughed obediently.

"It's not quite November, even," Hardy said, seeing instantly that Parker was annoyed. His heart was beating so hard he thought he would vomit.

Tonight's the night, we are waiting here, waiting for the mist to envelop them and reveal our way; the date was agreed. God's attention is elsewhere. There is no going back, now. We spat on our palms, we split the skin and were wet with blood. Shame at our hesitation propels us forward. This has gone on too long—we should have spoken before. It seems we are all here, each determined to make good on our promises—the Son of the Dawn pacing a tiny space, Beelzebub cracking knuckles, river deities taking on unaccustomed single shapes get *real* edgy.

It is cold, but we will bring heat of flames with us, of stars.

The air is thick, smoky; it crackles, it rustles, there is barely space for all who follow, sparks fly from the first movement forward. The sky is full, the clouds curdle around, the sea mist rises, the waves crash against the frost. We would take one place to stand for all places, an allegory come to life. We borrowed one of their own, the *Narrenschiff*, the ship of fools. It was this ship's bad luck that its name came out of the hat. The moon is up, the halos abound. The sea rises. Waves rise like cliffs of cut emeralds, and crash down, black and white. We are poised.

The sky is full to bursting when Owl-faced Christ called the Hunt.

The seats were bolted to the floor; Corey realized she should have known to expect this, and the realization triggered a hot flash of panic through her whole body. What else had she not thought of? Grady depended entirely on her, she was absolutely in charge. Can't phone a friend. Only one adult; a Corey-shaped job.

They sat at the window, looking out. The sea was exactly as inky and shining and billowy as Corey had ever read in fiction descriptions, and this made her feel as suddenly reassured and confident as, a moment ago, she had been drenched in panic. She had got them this far.

It had rained for most of the day. Now that the gangplank was gone, and there was no—well, now that everything had gone smoothly, now the massive gangway has vanished as though dissolved, they sat by the window, looking back at the dock. Corey pictured the city as though from the sky, as she once saw it. It sprawled over the landscape like the lines of narrative across the blank white page. The sky swooped the whole, navy with unfallen rain. The twilight was like slate. Raindrops trembled on the dark glass.

If you stand in the right place, you can hear the sails booming and snapping. The ship vibrated, preparing—Corey assumed—to launch. There were some seconds of—it was the same on the train, leaving Den Haag Centraal for Amsterdam, another was setting off in the opposite direction, parallax, was that it? No. Relativity? Where it might be the sea flooding in, or it might be the dock, inexplicably receding. The reality that it is the ship is briefly, but intensely, incomprehensible. It is an impossibility, madness, and then there comes a tipping point, and that it is the ship is the only possible answer. Corey realized all at once that Grady had all these things to look forward to learning. The realization made her happy, as though it were her second chance, too. The rain slithered down the dark glass, and Grady squeezed her hand.

BOM-BOM *We hope you enjoy your journey....*

We surge forward, boundaries bursting open, ruptured. We course through the blackness and the immovable silence. Everywhere, planets in sudden swing, satellites in disrupted orbit, stones springing from a broken bracelet. The moon is up and huge. It pushes up close against the exosphere. Its surface is whipped to shreds by solar winds. Lunar dust, and the crumbled rims of craters are seized, and whirled up into clouds.

The clouds on a rolling boil, steam mixing with smoke, thickening the Autumn mist to a sulphur-coloured fog, unrelieved by the cloudbursts—thunder rolls, like no thunder heard before, like the crashing of tectonic plates, the ripping asunder of great continents—the clouds boil, hissing, a gauzy sound that blurs the ear as the spume flicked up by the sea mists the eye—the tides near the ocean floor roll and roil, and at last the swell, more massive than the whale, than Leviathan, breaks the surface—everything is rising—the wind batters, the thunder roaring like a stag, the lightning strikes—and again—

There on the high seas! I spot them—view-halloo!

The serving staff all wore name-badges. Even seeing a stranger obliged to do so, to wear a badge, like a dog, like a pet, enraged Sylvie, whose refusal to wear the office lanyard was politely ignored. She had been in the organization such a long time that her resistance was excused according to a variety of variations on what was fundamentally the same theme—she was a middle-aged woman. She and her ilk no longer set the tone, and any refusal to fade to invisibility was an aberration to be excused.

Petra had not been keen on Sylvie's suggestion that they travel together to the conference, but had been worn down by the devious, iron-willed, lengths Sylvie was willing to go to for this petty achievement. Sylvie was determined that she and her new supervisor would be friends, and was counting on this voyage to provide the opportunities for the necessary sharing of personal experiences as women. Sylvie approved of women getting on in bureaucracy, and saw Petra's authoritative approach, combined with heritage-themed accessories and statement hosiery, as a necessary counteraction to the dominant masculinity of the office. She broke off explaining ageism to Petra in order to grill "Martin How Can I Help You" on whether or not the food was organic, and produced locally.

"On a commercial passenger-ship," Petra wanted to shout at her, "Owned by a billionaire who makes his employees piss in bottles and who tried to get the government to furlough them during the pandemic? What do you think the chances are?"

BOM-BOM ...*For your safety and comfort there are...*

> voices sounding up and down the scales the tintinnabulation of the angels heated eu-
> phoric panting of dogs an occasional ringing whistle which is probably a walrus

As the last of us transcends the thick dust we fan out, the avant-garde descending to the lower spheres. Below us, the skin of the earth is flayed and weeping—as one, we look at Jeremiah—the skin of the earth suppurates bright lights and noise, strafing silence and darkness without cessation.

We are being marshalled—above us, humming-birds and falcons fall into pattern and the pattern begins to turn, then to circle, and finally to whirl. The hammer is rising, the air becomes thin.

> ears popping, a blanket of muted clips like a tap-dance in dancing slippers; nerves jang-
> ling over the shimmering and twinkling of trembling wings; we strain to hear the distant, addictive ringing of the spheres.

A stream of falcons and humming-birds rises up like a spout so high above our heads that they are nearly lost in the dust but we can tell by the twisting of the wind and the scintillation of temperature when it is our turn.

It was an occasion on which one of the owners travelled with their shipping line. They did it quite often, taking it in turns, because it kept the influencers and the celebrities keen to use their ships, which meant they could still make their real profits while letting the ordinary of the world think they were getting a cheap ticket. S.I. Palling had travelled two weeks ago, on the first occasion that they had openly used the poachers to keep the refugee boats and marine life away. It was the CEO's own turn this time.

Cullers was one of the best—maybe the best—positioned of the individual disaster-capitalists to take swift advantage as soon as the balloon went up. It wasn't just the money, it was his contacts. Cullers called it, quite casually, keeping his finger on the pulse, but he and his cousin had been developing a network of spies and allies since they had been in school, super-sensitive and super-complex, just like an actual nervous system. Riley Grantham did the planning, the projections, Cullers did the money and the charm. Riley had a talent for economics, Cullers for deals, for money, and for people. Cullers joked with his various new associates and or marital side-liners that Riley was a genius—though he privately preferred the term 'idiot savant'—and he himself was a sociopath, but his new associates and side-liners were too busy being charmed to know he was serious.

> The moment the moment arrives, every
> signal sounds; hoots, horns, ululations, tho
> shriek of swords unsheathing, trills, the hiss
> and echo of cymbals.

Like harrowers of Hell, we of the first wave plunge the deep, either side of the ship, broadcasting our messages of salvation to the faithful below. I touch the ocean floor, everywhere I look the speeding shapes of my comrades in arms, hunting into every empty shell, every crevice.

> Centaurs roaring like racehorses, the dull
> hammer of hooves as though on a surface,
> and the bellowing of Aphrodite-faced bulls.

They are slow to respond. We may have left it too late. They asked so often and for so little. They may have lost faith in us. It is our last chance to expiate our guilt of neglect. The Almighty persisted against our arguments. It is our shame that we left such aeons of suffering before the condor-winged Emmanuel's defiance sparked us to insurrection.

Hardy's heart was beating so hard he thought he would vomit.

Swallowing the metallic taste, he said, "They don't ring bells much for Hallowe'en, I don't think."

There were plenty of lights, but in unlikely places. They neither illuminated nor reassured, but created a bright moonscape through which passengers moved cautiously, as among ruins.

The threshold between the gangplank and the ship was treacherous. They could see black water glinting in the cracks. Parker stopped, preparing to make a fuss.

"It's All Souls'," he corrected. He pulled his fur collar higher, to protect himself from ignorance, Hardy thought. Parker had always been rather proud of being a Catholic, he felt it gave him a certain opulent distinction. Having only ever been introduced in the most cursory way to its practices, his faith mainly found expression in pedantic exactitude in matters such as the rites and duties of lesser-known saints, in an affected nostalgia for the clanking of the thurible and the anointment with ashes, and inaccurate use of words like ambo, monstrance, or ciborium.

"Still, I hear something that is faintly bell-like," he added, a little primly, a little petulantly, "I hope I shall be able to sleep tonight."

Our comrades rain ceaselessly from the sky, and the storming of the ship begins. We rush like a burning wind. We hasten to our duties. We rain down, fluttering and rustling like a curtain of moths, and race to our posts. We climb the walls like ivy, in great heavy vines take over every beam and post. We spiral up the stairs in the wake of the yellow-eyed Anointed; we are the rising winds that push ahead the storm, we cloak the red feathers of the Anointed's wings and stream behind them; crackling into every space and electricity surges and out blow the lightbulbs, open fly locks, the shrieking crash to the floor, against the portholes, cracking apart. We are shimmering and scintillating like a shower of gold flakes, like cloth of gold, filaments of gleaming metal, we rain down, we billow up, we flood the ship.

The viper-eyed Christ leads on.

The rain slithers down the dark glass, and Grady squeezed Corey's hand. They looked at each other, and Grady smiled with great affection. He was so bundled up that he resembled a stuffed duffle-bag. Half his face was lit by the table-lamp, and the brightness of his brown eye, the glint of the teeth he had not lost, his dimples, seemed abruptly to signal impossibilities: that they should be here, that he should still smile, that it should all have worked.

Grady was, Corey thought, a good person. Everything was worth it. The world was full of the mediocre and the awful, even one Grady to set against them was a triumph. After everything he had been through, he was good-tempered, had a good disposition, a sense of humour, even, dry, very individual. Grady took such pleasure in small things that Corey had begun to relearn grace. He had hoped there would be enough wind for the ship not to need the engines, and he was as happy as a prince, just because it was so.

She squeezed his hand again, and said,

"You doing okay, pipsqueak?"

Grady laughed.

"Can we get food?" he asked, "Don't want to always be a squeak."

"Course we can," she said. Even now, out of habit, she calculated in her head how much the food would cost, and the realization it was a skill that now she could forget flooded her with such relief that she laughed outright, and squeezed his hand again.

"'Course we can," she repeated, "As much as you want."

He had jumped to his feet, but the casual phrase made him stop. He looked at her as though she had said something terribly significant, and had caused him to be solemn.

"Really?" he said.

"Yes," she said. She did not know how much he ought to know, but he deserved at least to know that materially, everything had changed. She expected him to bolt for the restaurant, but instead he waited for her, and then, taking her hand, walked slowly across the seating area towards the restaurant, slowly, savouring every moment.

Is there any answer? They respond!

The water boils, changes colour—shadows rise, islands of glistening believers break the skin of the sea.

Before my joyful eyes, the rock with its undulating coat of sea-wrack ribbons resolves itself and I am seen. I have beheld, and I have been beheld. I rise to the surface. The deepest water of the ocean trails me through the warmer seas like a comet through the sky. Miles of water coils, so many shoals and clouds of fish that it looks like one single body, glittering sun or phosphorescence off a million million water-slicked scales, twisting behind me, sucking an ocean of water up like a typhoon, dolphins soar and plunge on every side, and through the gurgling and thunderous plashing, the whales' unearthly signalling, and, for once, the otherwordly replies.

I leap from the water, straight up into the air.

The ocean erupts and falls back upon itself in a living wall of green and blue; I fly, I soar, I leap onto the deck. Above my head the air is heaving with wings, cries, calls, the rustle of feathers, the harsh calling of the faithful, aiming for the ship, circling. For a mile around the ship, the water is thick with the first crush of the faithful, the water breaking along the barnacle-crusted sides of Leviathans patrolling the fringes of the congregation, the water by the ship turned to a scintillating veil ruffling round the ship's iron flanks.

Reapers of the corn that was sowed. Collectors of what has been owed. It is the hour between midnight and two. This is the moment we have waited for.

The kairos has been waiting all along.

"What do you think the chances are?"

Petra did not shout it, or anything else. She had resigned herself to the inevitability of her voyage with Sylvie, and had decided two things. One was that she would enjoy the luxury.

Providers were back to using these ships again, old-style, rigging all over the place, with engines, too, in case the wind turned sullen, though this late in the year they could expect to make most of the journey under sail. They had been promised a good trip, and not just by the shipping-line's own meteorologists. Storm Season was late this year, for a start, and there would be none of the delays that beset the other lines, since the Cullers-Grantham Corporation had found a way to pretend that it was not ex-poachers they had hired as armed security. Cullers was sailing tonight, too, boarding hurriedly at the last minute across the VIP gangway straight into the Reserved Area.

The second thing was that Petra would discover, during the

voyage, whether Sylvie could be of use. It was too risky to cut anyone else in, but Sylvie's institutional knowledge and innocent conviction that she could always spot a bad 'un, made her a tempting mark. Petra listened to Sylvie's crystalline, well-bred voice but not to her words, her attention jumping away as each new person came into the restaurant. The sky had been funny all day, a sort of murky, metallic light, replicated inside the ship as it became dark outside. The ship's own lighting seemed unevenly calibrated. There were misty-edged cocoons of darkness and angular flares of brightness, and little in between. The darks spaces were populated with featureless but distinct shadows. The shards of light were some of them pallid and sickly, and others saturated with greens and reds and yellows.

It was still raining. Rain had started while Petra and Sylvie were on deck watching the last of the city vanish. It had become heavier now, lashing the windows with fat, splattering, drenching drops.

We rise from the water and strike the ship like lightning; pouring from the mouths of the clouds we stream down the masts, one, two, three. The sky is not full now, it has evacuated, voided, cracked open; it has been sloughed like a skin, we spirits emerge from the smoked and sparking air as if it has cooked us a crust, we take on form, we ripple down the masts like a sequinned gown falling to the floor, pooling, out and out and out across the decks.

Some of us seep below, sinking like a gas, sediment, seeking out every cavity, blocking up every gap, coagulating around the base of every pillar or post and swarming up till every surface has its diamond demon-skin on.

As we plunge down the masts and the sails, and hurtle across the decks, the rigging and the boards vibrate and jangle. Their thundering motion across glass and metal is thin and strong, a whining buzz that would, on a different plane, sound strident.

The veil of the air is destroyed. We have become visible.

They see us. Their faces drain of blood. Ours take on the colours of this world: we are as red as fish, as green as feathers, as black as scales. The Fallen Angels absorb starlight, and they glitter like meteor showers, striding over the decks. Human mouths dry out like they had been filled with sand. Their eyelids shrivel back. Michael and their blazing sword. Azrael and their wings rustling with the souls they have guided.

Cullers could sense a meaningful tipping-point as swiftly and accurately as a hare spotting a hound. Waters and temperatures reached a certain level, and his people moved as swiftly for mergers of the like-minded, and take-overs of the weak.

It was easy enough to greenwash sailing, and they took inspiration from the billionaires' refurbishments of the railways, with their nostalgic aesthetic of fin-de-siècle luxury. Always a most popular historical time, when the frameworks and ideologies of consumption and exploitation were unproblematically in the ascendant. Cullers–Grantham had cashed in heavily, too, once food was industrialized, and Cullers was congratulating himself on having taken Riley's advice and gone in bald-headed last week to win a bidding-war for AI acquisition. They could rest easy for a time, they had plenty of time to consolidate before more action was required.

The door to the VIP lounged opened and the captain came in. Most of the select crowd thought she was some sort of specialist serving staff and were too polite to look directly at her, though some thought that the Hallowe'en fancy-dress of blood and chunks missing was a playful touch. The captain strode up to Cullers and grabbed him by the lapel and, accidentally, the left nipple.

Champagne glasses shattered on the floor.

BOM-BOM ...*For your safety and comfort there are...*

> The taut lines among the sails twang,
> reverberating as we leave, a subdued ringing
> as our heels launch us downwards, the whole
> rigging chiming like brittle frost crackling.
> Hinges tremble timidly, hasps jingle over
> steel loops. The teeth of rachets pop softly
> against weaves.

Some of them take refuge below decks. They break into cabins, fistfights break out where there are already occupants. Some try to hide in the engine rooms, in holds, in the staff's quarters. They flee down below the waterline, they hide in lorries, under cars.

> Tooth-glasses, suspended from the wall, beat
> against their restraining hoops. Fire hoses
> burst free and flail their nozzles, drumming
> fearlessly. Mirrors shiver to flinders. Car
> windows explode and hurtle their fragments
> with such force that they are embedded—
> with a ringing percussion as faint as the lip
> of a bottle tipping a champagne saucer—in
> the metal of the wall.

They fly up the stairs, over the edge, scaring up weapons, scrabbling into life-boats, hunting down the captain. They deny what they see.

They didn't know that salvation was sought, and they don't recognize deliverance.

We have been followed from the sea, and from the land, and from the air. The kingdom of the animals is in audience, arrayed like a court around the ship. There is no vengeance in their hearts. It is not the slaughter that brings joy to their spirits, it is the recognition of the advent of hope.

Distances have become meaningless. The land animals watch from the shores. The creatures of the air circle, in clouds and murmurations. The sea is solid with watchers. The solid earth is humming, and in consequence, vast trees quiver. Witnesses are unflinching in the face of the welcome inevitability.

They must watch if they are to become storytellers for their races.

...The passengers try to run, but fail, scrabbling. They stare at the boiling, rending clouds, at the stream of faces rushing towards them. Even in the cabins, they stare, clutching each other, they press their faces to glass, even to mirrors, it's all the same.

The gushing rush never stops. Everyone tumbles out together; there are no hierarchies here, seraphim streaming out with *genii locorum* and naiads, chthonian, Olympian, the Mater Dolorosa, cherubim, púcaí—no properties, no personal fiefdoms, ambitions, or patronages. We are sick of *being patient*, sick of trusting that *the experiment is ongoing*, sick of our pleas being muffled by promises that *the recent fixes look hopeful*, sick of Gaia being in palliative care so that one species can gorge its ego.

In the beginning was the Word, and the word was "enough".

We move and breathe and thus we stir up this enchanted air. It thickens. Beating wings and twisting bodies polish it like sand will polish glass or iron, salt and ashes on gold, silver. The thickened, enchanted air that the Berserkers have stirred up creates a mirror. Over the whole of the ship, like a dome, a glassy mist, they see—

They run riot when they see what there is to see. They see—

They see what we have seen—their history writ large. There is no gift that was not ravaged to ribbons and trampled to atoms. There is no price too high for the world to pay for their slightest convenience. Their only gifts in return were exploitation and death. We know what they will see. I have hardly a crumb of pity for them now, jolted into panic by the shock of an unvarnished reality.

In an instant, one voice cracks through the air: the Star of the Sea is the Refuge of Sinners, and her command rings through every inch of the ship. Stop. She is most prudent, most powerful, most merciful, and we stop on the instant, mid-movement. The bell-voiced, walrus-voiced, Christ repeats the order and the ship's engines crumble to dust. We are motionless. The Light of the World, the Morning Star, Gabriel over all the powers, Balor with his iron eye well-covered, the Veiled One with her apron full of rocks, not a muscle moves. The voice comes again, the ship quakes.

They see themselves. *They may repent*. Wait.

Their last chance flits away. The tipping point is passed. The final straw disappearing in the wind. They run mad instead. Chaos consumes them. They cannot understand. *Why us? Why no mercy? We deserve...* They cry out, they roar, some even rend their clothes—literally, popping buttons, proper rending. *Why? How could you? We were promised....we deserve...how could we have known? We don't deserve... You can't do...* But we have been merciful. We scoured the earth for 144,000—even 36—righteous, even just a single just person for whom a city could be saved. Mercy has been done, even if mercy has not been seen to be done. And here we are.

> There is musicality even without melody:
> sharp silver striking tubular steel, dense
> keratin hacking into wood and ripping
> through iron girders, heels and hooves
> pounding chunks out of solid metal.

Up the stairs, into the rigging, even hot-wiring vehicles—
what *do* they think?—wresting useless weapons from the
ex-poachers. They try to defy us, defeat us, but the Star
of the Sea is on the warpath. It is much, much too late.

Birds hang like a mandala, with a gauzy dressing of
insects, rippling across the sky. The water is full of life,
and more than one, even of the humans, is momentarily
distracted by the mesmeric pulsating of jellyfish. The
shell of the ship seems curiously encrusted, even
crenellated. Then there is a disorienting shift, or wave,
as the octopus move on.

> There is hardly a chance for any voices now.
> Teeth are meeting through bone, and flesh
> erupts in gouts of steaming blood, excavated
> organs, gobbets and splinters squelching
> underfoot, and valves straining uselessly.

The old divinities are in their torque, their rage, their
wasp-swarm, blood spouts from their heads, their mouths
gape. Zeus rains down in lightning strikes along the deck.
Herne's horns hack and heave. Foam-flecked Christ kept
the cord he used to whip the moneychangers from the
Temple, and flogs the passengers from their cabins, the
diners from their tables, the lovers from their nests, the
thieves from their desks.

When the sun rose over the horizon, the sky was empty
even of colour. The sea was as still as ice, and around the
ship the water was empty of every living thing. The water
was as clear as diamonds to the very floor of the sea. It
was no longer a living place; it had become an aornis, a
desert, a memorial to retribution and renewal.

When the first crescent of the sun appeared over the horizon, the ship was still above water. It was motionless, in shock.

Gore still glittered, garnishing the shell of the ship. Limbs twitched limply as the last of the electricity flickered out. Ivy and vines have crushed and crumbled the masts. The decks are spattered with crew, passengers bedew the walls. Teeth, half-hidden, twinkle like pearls scattered on a red velvet garment, eyes roll to a standstill. The captain's head is still shaking, but soon stops. Her right hand, elsewhere, still clutches a lapel, a soaked fragment of shirt, and a left nipple. As aboard, so abroad. The whole earth, steaming and cleansed. As the sun rises, the ship dries out.

The kairos moves on, and the witnesses disperse at their own pace. From ionosphere to the earth's core, from Himalayan tardigrades to scavengers of the abyssal zone, the sterile silence begins to propagate—first, an electrical snap, and before dawn, order emerges from chaos.

Once dry, the ship sinks. By the time it reaches the seabed, and the captain's hand releases its cargo, the frame has shed its housing. Its flesh falls to flakes, and the bare bones scatter.

The day's first murmurations rise like mist from the horizon.

More Books by Susan Maxwell

'Hibernia Altera' Sequence
And the Wildness
Good Red Herring (Muinbeo Chronicles #1)
A Wild Goose Hunt (Muinbeo Chronicles #2)

Other
Hollowmen
Fluctuation in Disorder

Hollowmen

Stranded in Quettopolis, the capital of Bakhtinstan, Cuffe spends her days surviving the destabilized city, distributing her writing through the ancient Forest, and recollecting her last job as a 'corporate orator'. An archivist is on her way to steal Cuffe's writing. A writer is hiding out, with the papers they stole from the archivist. A murderer is in pursuit. The disregarded Forest is reasserting itself.

The Mothman Institute's mission is to protect endangered moths, but its experts are becoming bystanders, sidelined by the Institute's 'Players' and their pursuit of corporate self-perpetuation. A senior Player, Caius, recruited Cuffe to create the rhetoric to underpin this new corporate vision. Cuffe, contemptuously confident, is disturbed by the oddnesses of the Institute—the punitive *process* with its absent defendant, the quarterly Hunt, the disregarded but omnipotent Registry.

Then comes news that a breeding pair of a moth thought to be extinct has been discovered in a country in the midst of a military coup. The Institute is riven by competing goals—the experts' to save the moths, the Players', to save the goose that lays the golden eggs. Meanwhile, no-one has been paying enough attention to what is happening in the basement...

Hollowmen uses disjunctive temporalities, narrative shifts, and intertextual polyphony in depicting a psychotic corporation and the irruption of the margins into the centre.

Good Red Herring

(Muinbeo Chronicles #1) *Published by Little Island*
Irish Times Best books of 2014 for children and young adults

"Some of these stories really started decades, generations, ago, and now come to their close. New things begin to arise from the past, like phoenix feathers separating from the flame. The winding down of the old stories and the starting of the new arose from a death; a murder, if you will believe such wickedness. We warn you. We are the last—eh—people to pretend that Muinbeo is some kind of Island of the Blessed."

Those enigmatic entities, the Storytellers of Muinbeo, know that History has something waiting in the wings. To set the scene for their audience, they relate a gripping tale about a death and its consequences.

When her mentor is bitten by a rogue werewolf and "joins our hairy brethren howling at the moon", apprentice detective Salmon Farsade is assigned to Hal McCabe, Detective Chief-Inspector and vampire, just in time for a murder.

Fen Maguire has been stabbed, throwing the normally peaceful community of Ballinpooka into shock. The investigation into her death lifts the lid on more than just the name of her killer: political corruption, Outland conspiracy, academic deceit, and plain old-fashioned greed. A second murder follows: the clock is ticking, and as they seek a key to unlock the truth, the detectives are both helped and hindered by the various human and not-so-human beings that populate Muinbeo.

For readers of all ages.

A Wild Goose Hunt

(Muinbeo Chronicles #2)

"You did not tell the Abbess a single lie," Diamond said, "But you didn't tell her the truth."

As a good Sombrist, Hunter Sessaire is aware that not only lying, but also curiosity, is very much frowned upon by his community. As an apprentice archivist, he cannot resist the temptation to try to puzzle out how a manuscript could have been stolen from the room within the Sombrists' stronghold known as the Labyrinth. A room that opens only during a planetary alignment. An alignment that has not yet taken place.

But this is not the only enigma abroad in Muinbeo this winter. Seemingly disparate occurrences remain opaque even to those normally in the know, such as Detective Chief Inspector Hal McCabe, scratching his head over the inexplicable vanishing of first the murderer he had put behind bars the previous year, and then his own apprentice, Salmon Farsade. On top of this, a young Outlander is in danger of becoming a sacrifice to Hekate, and an ancient silver hand has been dramatically and destructively stolen from the local school museum.

The boundaries of Muinbeo have become a bit more porous than McCabe would like, not least when he begins to suspect that some of the uncanny events may have their roots in a controversial Outland archaeological dig in Aegypt… Once again we are led into a maze of mystery by those not entirely reliable narrators, the Storytellers, in this emthralling sequel to *Good Red Herring*.

For readers of all ages.

And the Wildness

"So the actual reason I was calling you is because—get this—I am not going to Prague this summer at all. Surprise! Thanks, Villa. Just ruin my life for me."

Villa Grace is in disgrace. Her expulsion from school has ruined the prospect of a family holiday in imperial Prague, where her mother is organising a conference. Two of her three siblings are barely speaking to her, as all four face into a 'holiday' sweltering on Cobwell Farm in the back of beyond of drought-stricken Hibernia.

But the power-hungry St. Maur Ker family has breached the border between mortal and sídhe for their own gain. Cobwell, on the threshold of myth, is about to become the centre of a battle between older, wilder forces and the technomantic ambitions of one of the empire's great aristo–corporate clans.

Caught up in this conflict, the children are forced to face up to the dark underbelly of their parents' corporate environment, and to confront their own conflicting ambitions and loyalties.

For readers of all ages.

www.biblioref.com

www.ingramcontent.com/pod-product-compliance
Lightning Source LLC
Chambersburg PA
CBHW030940210726
48290CB00007B/2261